Francisco smoothed the hair back from her face. His eyes were black pools in the darkness. "I make no promises . . . to anyone," Francisco said. Then he added with a quick smile, "But I believe in love most definitely!"

Kit sighed. "Sometimes, I don't know. I mean, maybe love is just one of those things that doesn't last, no matter how much you want it to."

"You expect too much, Kit. If you try to possess love, it will die—like a butterfly in captivity. You must take it as it comes . . . then, when it is ready to fly away, you won't be sad." Francisco kissed her gently. "Tonight, I am in love. Maybe tomorrow, too." He shrugged. "Then, who knows?"

Kit allowed him to kiss her again, this time more deeply. Francisco was right. She wasn't going to let herself think about the future . . . or even the past. She was just going to enjoy this moment while it lasted.

SENIORS

TOO MUCH, TOO SOON

SMART ENOUGH TO KNOW

WINNER ALL THE WAY

AFRAID TO LOVE

BEFORE IT'S TOO LATE

BEFORE IT'S TOO LATE
by Eileen Goudge

To Helen Pyne for her unending enthusiasm
and hard work.

Published by
Dell Publishing Co., Inc.
1 Dag Hammarskjold Plaza
New York, New York 10017

Laurel-Leaf Library ® TM 766734, Dell Publishing Co., Inc.
ISBN: 0-440-90542-7
RL: 6.2
Printed in the United States of America

First printing—February 1985

Chapter One

"Close your eyes," Kit said.

She snuggled closer to Justin. The rock they were sitting on formed a slight hollow, like a pair of cupped hands. It felt warm against the backs of her legs and her wet bikini bottom. Below, the gray-green water of the cove reflected the late afternoon sun in a thousand glittering pinpoints.

"How come?" Justin asked.

"Don't ask. It's a surprise."

Justin leaned back against the rock behind him. "Okay . . . they're closed."

Kit wound her arms around him, pressing close in a slow, searching kiss. Justin's lips tasted salty from their swim. Her fingers crept up the back of his neck, where his hair had sprung loose in a tangle of damp curls.

Justin was smiling as they drew apart—that adorable crooked smile she loved so much. His calm gray eyes held a vaguely bewildered look, as if he weren't quite sure where she was coming from.

He often got that slightly dazed look when she did something outrageous or unexpected, Kit thought. Her best friend Elaine had once compared Kit's effect on Justin to that of a hurricane hitting an island at 200 miles per hour. She'd only been teasing, of course, but in some ways it was true.

Because they were so different, Kit was always amazed at how well they got along. She thought of herself as the emotional type, whereas Justin was more logical and serious. He never hurried into anything. Whether he was deciding something as important as where he wanted to go to college or simply what flavor of ice cream he was going to have when they went to Baskin Robbins, Justin traveled in a sure, straight line, confident that the direction he was headed in was the right one for him.

Kit was never that sure of herself. She felt so scattered sometimes—as if she might fly apart in a dozen different directions. Take dancing, for instance. When she danced, she was happy and would forget about everything else. But when she was with Justin, like now, there was nowhere else she'd rather be.

"That wasn't much of a surprise," Justin

said, tightening his arm about her bare shoulders. "I knew you were going to kiss me."

"That's because you always open your eyes at the last minute. Don't deny it. I saw you."

"If you saw me, that means you had yours open, too." He regarded her soberly, but his wide-set gray eyes sparkled with a teasing light. "Besides, I *like* looking at you. You're so pretty, Kit."

Kit could feel herself blushing. She never knew quite how to respond when Justin told her she was pretty. Should she act surprised, as if she didn't think so herself? Or blasé, as if she'd known it all along?

The truth was, she didn't always think she was so great-looking. At her best, when she was dressed up to go out on a date, hair and makeup perfect, wearing, say, her red minidress with the black patent-leather belt, she might give herself an eight and a half, maybe even a nine. Other times, though, like when she looked in the mirror first thing in the morning, Kit didn't think she rated above a zero.

A lot of people had told her she looked like Goldie Hawn, because of her big blue eyes and mop of blond curls. She also had a kind of heart-shaped mouth that looked as if it were puckered in a permanent kiss—which to Kit's embarrassment, boys often mistook as a standing invitation. One of the reasons she loved Justin so much was because he cared for her as a whole person. While he appreciated the way she looked, he was concerned about what went on inside, too.

Kit threw a mysterious look at him. "The kiss wasn't the *real* surprise. Just a preview of coming attractions."

"Okay, what is it? You've been acting mysterious about something ever since we got to the beach. The suspense is killing me."

Kit took a deep breath. Excitement swelled inside her like a bubble threatening to burst. She'd been dying to tell him ever since she'd gotten the good news, but she'd wanted to wait until the right moment, when they were alone. Up until now, they'd been with Danny and Alex ever since Danny had picked them up in his truck to take them to the beach. It was Kit who had suggested to Justin that the two of them swim over to the rocky side of the cove, which was inhabited mainly by sea gulls.

Squinting as she peered across the milky gray-green water, Kit could see Alex now—a flash of red in her cranberry-colored one-piece as she sprinted down the narrow strip of beach with Danny in hot pursuit. Kit smiled. Danny would have to run a lot faster than that if he wanted to catch up with Alex. . . .

Kit turned back to Justin. "I did it," she said. "I finally convinced her."

Justin blinked in confusion. "Convinced who?"

"My mother, of course." She twirled her

4

finger around one of the dark-blond curls that dipped over his forehead, giving it a gentle tug. "Don't you remember? The trip to Tahoe?"

They'd been talking about it for ages. An old college friend of her mother's, Sandra Cunningham, owned a cabin on the north shore of Lake Tahoe, and she'd invited Kit and Janice up for the summer. Mom would be working though, except for a ten-day vacation she thought she might take there in August. The rest of the time it would be practically empty, since Sandra worked during the day and spent most nights over at her boyfriend's. Kit and Justin had talked about how great it would be if they could go up there themselves, just the two of them, for a week or two. The problem was getting her mother to agree. True, Sandra was the official chaperone, but since she was almost never home, Justin and Kit would have the cabin to themselves. Janice was the liberal type . . . but even liberal had its limits.

Kit's argument had been that if it was okay for her mom to go on a trip with one of her boyfriends, as she frequently did, why should it be any different for *her*?

"Because, *you're* not *me*," Janice had answered. "I'm your mother, remember?"

Sometimes Kit had a hard time remembering that fact. Janice often acted more like an older sister than a mother. Occasionally, she could even be downright irresponsible, like staying out all night when she was in love with

5

some new guy.

For the most part, though, they got along. Like friends, they teased each other a lot and borrowed each other's clothes. Kit could talk to Janice about almost anything, even boys, and Janice usually understood. She'd had enough stormy relationships of her own to be able to empathize.

In this case, that had been part of the problem, too. Even though Janice didn't really mind that Kit and Justin would be spending a week together without a chaperone, she'd been afraid they might do something stupid, like run off to Reno and get married, the way she had when she was seventeen. It took weeks of pleading on Kit's part to convince her mother that she would never do anything so irresponsible. Besides, Kit didn't want to *marry* Justin, she just wanted to be able to spend some time alone with him before they both went away to college.

Now here was Justin, acting as if they'd never even discussed the trip in the first place! Kit felt a twinge of uneasiness. She could hardly believe he had forgotten something as important as this. Then, an even worse thought occurred to her—what if he'd changed his mind about wanting to go?

"Sure I remember," Justin said. He looked down, suddenly absorbed in picking at a tuft of seaweed poking up through a crack in the rock.

The way he replied—as though the trip were a dentist's appointment he'd just remembered—made Kit feel twice as uneasy as before. "You don't sound very excited. I thought you wanted to go."

"I do . . . I mean, I did."

"And you don't anymore?"

Justin was silent. As she took in his blank expression, the bubble of excitement she'd felt about the trip dissolved into a hard lump of fear.

"What is it, Justin?" she asked hesitantly.

Justin looked up at her. His expression had gone from blank to apologetic. The skin along the top of his nose and the sharp ridges of his cheekbones was red from the sun. Now his face turned even redder.

"I'm sorry, Kit. I should have let you know sooner. But, well, I've been waiting for the right moment to tell you—I got a full-time job. I'll be working all summer long."

The hard lump inside her sank into her stomach with a sickening jolt. Kit slipped out from under his arm, hunching forward as she hugged her knees to her chest. She couldn't believe what was happening. How could he *do* this to her?

"How long have you known?" she asked, struggling to control her disappointment.

"Only since yesterday. Believe me, Kit, I would've told you right away. Except . . . I wasn't sure how you'd take it. After all the plans we made, that is."

"I don't get it," she said slowly. "What about the job you already have?" They both worked part-time at Gennaro's Pizza Parlor after school and on Saturday mornings. Wasn't that enough?

"It's not the same," Justin explained. "This is a *real* job. My Uncle Van knows the professor who's in charge of the biology department at Stanford. He needed a lab assistant . . . and I said I'd do it."

"Just like that? You said yes, without even having to think about it . . . or . . . or talk to someone about it?"

Kit felt his light touch against her shoulder, but she refused to turn around. She pulled her legs in tighter against her chest, propping her chin on her knees as she stared out at the choppy water. She felt so betrayed.

"Kit, it's a great opportunity. How could I say no? You of all people should realize how much I want to be a doctor. It's a chance to get the kind of experience I need. Also, the job will look good on my record when I apply to med school."

Kit wanted to understand; she really did. She knew how important it was for Justin to follow his dream of becoming a doctor. She felt the same way about dancing. All week, she'd been anxiously waiting to hear if the video tape her dance teacher had sent to the Juilliard scholarship committee was going to qualify her for an audition with the committee.

That was just it, she thought. What if she *did* get accepted to Juilliard? It would mean that next fall she'd be three thousand miles away. This summer was the last chance she and Justin would have to be together. They'd talked about it; he knew how she felt. She'd thought he felt the same way.

What hurt most of all was that he hadn't even discussed it with her before accepting the job. And what about all the other plans they'd made? The trip to Tahoe was only one of the things they'd discussed. There was also the Sierra Club camping trip they'd planned to go on with Danny and Alex. And what about the scuba diving lessons they'd signed up for at the YMCA? Not to mention all the days they would've spent just hanging out together, enjoying their own special closeness.

"What about us?" Kit asked, feeling very small all of a sudden. "This was supposed to be *our* summer. What about all the things we were going to do together?"

"I'm sorry, Kit. I wish there was enough time for us to . . . well, for everything. But we'll still see each other. We'll still do things. Besides, summer won't be here for a long time. Why worry about it now?"

Kit nodded, her throat aching as she struggled to hold back the tears. Fat chance they'd still see each other. When they were both working at Gennaro's they'd always managed to grab a few minutes together in the kitchen.

Now they wouldn't even have that. With Justin working all week at some lab and her working on the weekend, they'd be lucky if they saw each other at all.

Kit paused as it all sank in. With Justin, she'd always felt as if she came first. She needed to have someone she could feel that way with, since Janice didn't always make her feel secure about that.

Kit knew her mom loved her, but it was often a distracted love. Janice was busy with her job and her boyfriends. She had a habit of absorbing herself in whomever she was dating at the moment. Like a chameleon, Kit thought, remembering the health food kick her mom had gone on when she was going with Barry, the body builder. And the time Janice had taken up guitar lessons when she was living with Hugh, who was really into music.

Her father was the same, in a different way. Because he had married again, and lived with Vi and her two daughters, Kit was no longer a major part of his new life, not really. When she was over at their house, she felt like the piece to a puzzle that doesn't really fit, no matter how many different ways you try to wedge it in.

The closest thing Kit had to sisters were her friends—Alex, Elaine and Lori. Her better-than-best friends. She knew they loved her as much as she loved them, but still . . . they had their own families, too, as well as boyfriends they would be spending the summer with.

Justin was first with Kit in so many ways, she'd always just assumed she came first with him, too. He was her first real boyfriend; the first boy she'd trusted enough to let down her barriers with . . .

Now . . . she wondered if she hadn't been wrong from the very beginning. Maybe Justin didn't love her nearly as much as she'd imagined. Obviously, this summer job meant more to him than she did.

"We should be getting back," Kit said. The breeze blowing off the cove had turned slightly chilly, and the only thing she had on was her bikini. She forced a tight laugh. "Alex and Danny'll think we drowned."

"Kit." Justin's hand was warm against her back. "Please . . . I want you to understand."

"I do, Justin." She understood all too well.

"Look, mid-term break starts next Monday. I have to spend part of it with my grandparents in San Diego, but we'll still have the last week."

Kit whipped around suddenly. "Let's just not talk about it, okay?" She stood up. The breeze caught a damp strand of hair, flinging it against her cheek. "I'm swimming back."

"Kit . . . wait." Justin stood up beside her, reaching out to put his arms around her.

Kit was afraid that if she let him hold her, she would weaken. She would allow herself to pretend he loved her the same as before. She didn't want that to happen.

Ducking to avoid his embrace, she took a

step backwards. Her foot slipped on the wet rock, and she lost her balance. She would've fallen flat on her face if she hadn't caught the weight of the fall against one knee. A flash of pain jolted through her. She rolled into a sitting position, clutching her leg. Her knee stung where she'd scraped it. Blood oozed from the raw scrape and trickled down her shin.

Then Justin was beside her, cradling her in his arms. "Kit, are you okay?"

"Sure, I'm okay," she cried. "Can't you see how okay I am?" She was on the verge of tears, but she choked them back, feeling them form a knot at the back of her throat.

"Let me see." Justin lifted her leg gently onto his lap.

He was wearing a pair of bright yellow swim trunks. In spite of her anger, Kit couldn't help noticing how the muscles in his stomach rippled as he moved. He had the kind of body a basketball player would envy—long and rangy, with a loose-limbed way of moving.

He bent to examine the scrape, his hands cradling her leg so tenderly, so carefully. He would make a good doctor, she thought with a stab. Someday, there she'd be, bleeding to death in the middle of the road after some horrible car wreck. She'd open her eyes, and there *he* would be, bending over her in a white coat, with a stethoscope around his neck.

"Don't worry," Justin would say. "I won't let you die. I love you too much . . . more than anything."

Kit's fantasy was ruptured when the real-life Justin spoke up: "I'm sorry you got hurt, Kit. But I'm not sorry I took the job. Don't you see? I had to. It's my *future*."

"What about right now?" Kit cried. "Doesn't that count at all?"

"Sure it does. Only I can't stand still. I have to be thinking ahead. Don't you feel that way about dancing?"

She hated it when he tried to turn an argument around on her. Why did he have to be so logical? "I think about dancing a lot, but not all the time," she said. "Besides, I figure I'll have the whole rest of my life to be a dancer. But this summer . . . I wanted it to be something really special. A time I'd always remember, even when"—her voice caught, and she blinked back the tears that filled her eyes—"when we're far apart."

Justin frowned. "You make it sound as if we won't see each other at all. That's silly, Kit."

Now he was calling her silly! That really stung.

Disentangling herself from him, Kit struggled to her feet. She hobbled over to the edge of the rock, putting a safe distance between them before she allowed herself to turn and face him. The wind caught her from behind, blowing her hair around her face, raising goose pimples along her spine.

"Maybe we *won't*!" she cried. "Maybe you'll

13

be so busy you'll forget all about me!"

Justin's jaw went tight; his cloud-gray eyes darkened. Obviously, he thought she was making a big deal out of nothing. He didn't care how she felt. Why did he have to be so sure of himself, anyway? Why couldn't he forget about the future just for a little while? She didn't expect him to give up his dream of becoming a doctor, any more than she would've wanted to give up her own dreams. It would be wonderful if they both got what they wanted . . . someday.

Kit couldn't help feeling that Real Life wouldn't begin until she entered college. Real Life meant living away from home, making decisions about the future, and a lot of other scary things. Not that she wasn't excited about college. She was! She just didn't want to rush into it the way Justin did, shoving aside everything else like outgrown toys.

They stood there, staring at each other for a long, speechless moment. But Justin's face was impassive, his expression remote, as if he were thinking how strange it was they'd ever fallen in love in the first place.

Kit thought about the time before they'd begun dating, when she'd tried to get his attention, and he'd acted as if she were invisible. Later, she convinced herself that she'd imagined the whole thing. But maybe she hadn't. Maybe Justin had always had his mind on other things . . . things that were more important to him than her.

Yet . . . in the same instant, she couldn't forget his tenderness toward her the rainy night she'd showed up unexpectedly at his house, miserable about the fight her parents were having over her. He'd been genuinely concerned about her feelings then. And afterwards, when they'd made love for the first time, she'd felt so close to him. She'd never felt that close to anyone before . . .

It was hopeless, Kit thought. She couldn't make herself stop loving Justin . . . even if he'd begun to stop loving her.

With a tiny choked cry, she turned and dove into the water, feeling it close about her like a cold fist.

Chapter Two

Alex darted over to Kit as she was coming up the beach. "Kit, what happened? You look like you got attacked by Jaws!"

Kit stared down at her leg. The stinging had stopped, but blood had mingled with seawater, streaking her leg from the knee down in pale pink. It looked worse than it felt. What hurt more was the ache inside her.

"I'm okay," she said, hobbling over to their blanket and flopping down. "It wasn't a shark . . . just a rock."

"You were attacked by a ravenous rock?"

Kit looked up as Alex handed her a dry towel. Her friend's dark, almond-shaped eyes danced with mischief. Kit giggled in spite of herself.

That was Alex for you. Always cracking jokes, making you laugh when you were at your lowest. She had a talent for lifting Kit's spirits when she was down either by teasing her out of it, or forcing her to stop feeling sorry for herself.

Alex stretched out beside Kit, lying on her side with her elbow cocked to support her head. She reminded Kit of one of those girls in suntan lotion ads. Her skin seemed to glow, a rich honey-brown, against her red one-piece. She had the kind of body, lean and compact, where absolutely nothing jiggled when she moved. Like a gymnast, Kit thought, only Alex did most of her gymnastics from the end of a diving board. She'd won several regional championships and Kit was sure nothing would stop her friend from making the Olympic team someday.

Alex had her head tilted so that her hair fanned out on one side in a glossy dark flag. Her dark eyes regarded Kit with a mixture of amusement and concern.

"Something's wrong—besides your leg, I mean," she observed. Alex had a way of getting right down to basics that was as brisk as the way she moved. "Listen, if you want to talk about it, it looks like our boy scouts are going to be busy for a while building a fire."

Kit glanced over to where Justin and Danny were stacking driftwood in a pile. Justin had thrown on an old sweatshirt and a pair of cutoffs. Danny's blond head bent close to Justin's in conversation. Kit was too far away to hear what they were talking about, but it must have been funny, because Justin let out a loud laugh. Kit winced. Here she was, suffering from a broken heart, and Justin was *laughing* . . . as if nothing had happened.

She turned away. Watching Justin—the easy way he loped across the sand with a load of driftwood tucked under one muscular arm—was too painful. She scooped up a handful of warm sand, letting it trickle through her fingers.

"Did you and Justin have some kind of fight?" Alex prodded.

"Not really," Kit said. "I wouldn't call it an actual fight."

"You mean like Justin trying to take a bite out of your leg, for instance?" Alex kidded.

"Cut it out, Alex. This is serious. I think I'm losing Justin. Or," she sighed, "maybe I never had him to begin with." Kit dropped onto her back, staring up at the sky which was beginning to darken now that the sun was sinking into the ocean. The sound of the waves reminded her of every sad movie about breaking up she'd ever seen. "Do you ever get the feeling when you're with Danny that there's someplace else he'd rather be, besides with you?"

"Yeah, in the water," Alex replied. Danny was a diver, too—one of the many things they had in common. "Sometimes," she added, sobering, "we both get in each other's hair. Then if we didn't do something else, stuff apart from each other, we'd probably end up killing each other."

"I don't mean how you feel *sometimes*," Kit said. "I mean like . . . *all* the time. What if Danny had the choice of being with you all summer or, say, going off on some safari to Africa?"

Alex's dark eyes widened. "Is Justin going to Africa on a safari? Is that what this is all about?"

"No, silly, of course not. I was just using that as an example. *What if.*"

"Well, if Danny wanted to go on a safari I'd probably beg him to take me with him." She grinned, her eyes crinkling up their tipped up corners. "I've always wanted to bag a rhinoceros."

"Alex!"

"Okay, I was only joking." Alex sat up and began fishing in her straw beach bag. She dug out a purple sweat shirt and pulled it on over her head. Across the front it said: "When God Made the World, She Did a Pretty Good Job." "The point is, you can't go by the way Danny and I do things, or the way we feel about each other. We're different people from you and Justin." She peered at Kit, pushing back her bangs, which were blowing around in the breeze. "What happened between you guys, anyway?"

"He just told me he got a job for the summer, working in a laboratory. I probably won't see

19

him all summer!"

"Is that what he said—that he wouldn't see you all summer?"

"Not exactly. But don't you understand? It doesn't matter what he says. It's what he's *doing*. He didn't even bother to discuss it with me first. He just went ahead and accepted the job . . . even after all the plans we made to be together this summer. He doesn't care how I feel."

"I'm sure that's not true, Kit." Alex touched Kit's arm. "Justin loves you. Maybe he just has a different way of showing it."

Kit watched a sea gull float by on an invisible stream of wind. *Did* Justin love her? she wondered. Only a few hours ago she'd thought so. Now . . . well, she wasn't so sure.

"He loves his dog, too," she said. "And his Billy Joel collection. And his Levi's jean jacket with the patches."

"I don't see how you can compare yourself to a dog . . . or a record collection," Alex said dryly. "Don't you think that's going a little far?"

"Maybe," Kit admitted. She dug her toes into the sand, her gaze wandering back to Justin. He and Danny had finally gotten a fire started, though it was mostly smoke at this point. The sharp, sweet smell drifted towards her, a summer smell she always associated with beach parties and summer barbecues and

Fourth of July celebrations. Something pulled at her heart as she thought again of all the things she'd be missing with Justin. "I guess what I'm trying to say is . . . you can love a lot of things or people that aren't necessarily all that important to you."

"You don't think you're important to Justin?"

"Not important enough."

"Hey, Alex!" Danny called over. He was kneeling in front of the Styrofoam cooler, rummaging inside. "Where's the hot dogs? Did we forget to bring them?"

Alex hopped to her feet and ran over. She fished a plastic bag out of the cooler, dangling it in front of Danny's face. "There. They were right in front of your nose the whole time." She swatted him playfully on the arm. "What would you do without me?"

Danny clutched his chest in mock alarm. "I'd croak! I'd dry up and blow away like a tumbleweed!"

Watching them clown around, Kit felt a stab of envy. They might look like a mismatched pair—Alex, with her dark half-Japanese features, and blond, blue-eyed Danny, the all-American hero type—but they really made a good team, despite all their teasing. They obviously depended on each other. She doubted that Danny would've taken a full-time summer job without consulting Alex first.

Kit found a skewer for her hot dog and sat down in front of the fire. She wasn't really hungry—it was just something to do. Justin was hunkered down across from her, but he made no move to get up and come around to where she was sitting.

Their eyes met as one of the logs caved in, sending up a shower of sparks. They stared at each other through the swirling curtain of sparks. Justin was giving her what Kit called his "Mr. Spock" look—deadpan except for a slightly puzzled frown, as if she were an equation he couldn't figure out.

Kit was the first to look away. She couldn't bear it—this awful distance that had come between them. Beside her, Alex and Danny sat close together, wrapped in one blanket, their sizzling hot dogs nearly touching. Alex had her head snuggled against Danny's shoulder. He was whispering something in her ear.

Tears filled Kit's eyes. As if from a distance, she heard Justin cry: "Kit!" He sounded concerned . . . desperate almost.

An image flashed across her mind of Marlon Brando in his torn T-shirt yelling, "Stella!" in *A Streetcar Named Desire*, one of her favorite old movies. It was the scene where Brando realizes how crazy he is about his wife, right after they've had a big fight. Kit's heart leaped. Had Justin finally realized how much he cared for her?

"Kit!" he said again.

She looked at him; his face was a blur through the tears that clouded her eyes. "Yes?" she piped hopefully.

Justin was pointing into the fire. Kit glanced down at her stick. At the end of it, where her hot dog had been, was a charred lump.

"That's what I was trying to tell you," he said. "Your hot dog was on fire."

Chapter Three

"I know what you mean about Justin," Elaine said as they were riding to school on the bus Monday morning. "I feel that way with Carl sometimes. When he's working at his computer, it's like he's on another planet."

Kit sat squashed between Elaine and a spring that was sticking up through the torn seat. The thing about school buses, she'd observed, was that they were all about a hundred years old; the one she and Elaine were riding on looked like it had been in use since the days of covered wagons.

Kit and Elaine usually rode their bikes to school, but this morning Kit had discovered that hers had a flat tire. On top of that, she'd been running so late she hadn't even had time to pick out a decent outfit to wear. At the last minute she'd thrown on a pair of jeans and a slightly wrinkled T-shirt she'd found in a heap

24

at the foot of her bed. She hadn't even had time to comb her hair after taking out her curlers, and the result was a mass of curls that looked as frazzled as she felt.

She glanced over at Elaine with a sigh of exasperation. Elaine looked as calm and cool as if she were riding in a limousine. Nothing ever appeared to ruffle Elaine very much. Kit envied her friend's incredible talent for being organized—one of the reasons, besides being brilliant, that Elaine was a straight-A student. She never appeared to hurry, but she was always on time. She never waited until the last minute, as Kit often did, to do her homework or finish an essay paper. Elaine was . . . well, if Kit didn't love her so much, she would probably hate her. Except that Elaine was too nice for anyone to hate, in spite of how infuriatingly organized she was.

Today Elaine was wearing a pleated green skirt and white shirtwaist blouse, with knee socks and loafers. Her shoulder-length brown hair was held back by a headband. Brown eyes the color of nutmeg peered out from behind a pair of tortoiseshell glasses that were half the size of her face.

Kit knew that Elaine didn't think of herself as pretty, and that was one reason she didn't go out of her way to wear makeup and eye-catching clothes. But in Kit's opinion, Elaine had something even better than dazzling looks—she was funny and interesting and

25

. . . well, *together.* Kit's favorite story when she was little had been *The Three Little Pigs.*

Elaine reminded her of the smart one, the one who built his house out of bricks so the Big Bad Wolf couldn't blow it over. It was no wonder she'd been voted "Most Likely to Succeed" on the Senior Poll.

Even so, Kit knew that, deep down, Elaine worried as much as she did about boys. That was why Kit felt so comfortable confiding in Elaine about the rift that had developed between Justin and her over his summer job. Elaine had enough problems with her own boyfriend, Carl, to understand what Kit was going through.

"I wonder why it is that girls seem to worry more about these kinds of things than boys," Kit said with a sigh. "I mean, it seems like we spend nine-tenths of our time agonizing over the problems we have with our relationships, but if we asked our boyfriends about it, they'd say, 'What problems?' Guys always seem to be too busy playing football . . . or thinking about their future careers to worry that much about us."

Elaine nodded in agreement. "I think it all dates back to the invention of the telephone."

"What's the telephone got to do with it?"

"Well, I have this theory that the telephone is where all the worrying starts. I mean, think about it. From the very beginning, you're at the boy's mercy. You wait around endlessly for the

26

phone to ring, hoping it'll be that certain boy you're dying to go out with. And every time it does ring, you practically jump out of your skin . . . even though it's never for you. It's always some dumb friend of your sister or somebody selling magazine subscriptions. Meanwhile, with all of that waiting around, your nerves are shot and you become a hopeless wreck!"

Kit laughed, remembering all too well what it was like to sit around at home, waiting for the phone to ring. "Remember that crush I had on Chuck Hadley when we were sophomores?"

"Do I ever! He's all you ever talked about for a whole semester."

"There was this one time when Alex talked me into calling *him* up, since it didn't look as if he was ever going to call me."

Elaine grinned. "That sounds like something Alex would do."

"Well, it didn't exactly work out the way she planned. I was supposed to ask him to the Sadie Hawkins dance, but in the end I chickened out and asked him if he had the homework assignment for algebra. Afterwards, I was glad I hadn't asked him to the dance—he didn't even remember who I was! When I told him, he said, 'Oh, yeah . . . are you the one who sits behind Dave Bender?' He'd gotten me mixed up with Cathy McNeil!"

Elaine braced herself against the side of the bus as it rounded the corner onto Glenwood Avenue, swaying dangerously. Her glasses had slipped down her nose, and she poked them back into place.

"Sometimes I wonder why we bother," Elaine commented with a dry laugh. "Half the time it seems so hopeless."

"The trouble is—the other half of the time makes it all worthwhile. I can't stop thinking about all the great times Justin and I have had together. I wish it could be that way forever. . . ."

"Nothing lasts forever," Elaine pointed out logically. "Not even things that are supposed to."

"I know," Kit replied, thinking about her parents' divorce. "With Justin, I just want to make the most of the time we have left. Before it's too late. Before we have to say good-bye in September. Who knows?—I might be going to college in New York City."

Elaine's brown eyes lit up. "Did you hear from Juilliard?"

"Not yet. Mrs. Rosen is expecting a letter any day announcing the scholarship finalists. I think the video tape she sent of me was pretty good, but I don't know . . . there are probably five thousand kids who are better than me."

"You shouldn't think that way, Kit. You've got real talent."

Kit blushed. "You're just saying that."

Elaine cast her an outraged look. "I'm your best friend. Would I lie to you?"

"Yes!" Kit cried, adding with a giggle, "That's

what best friends are for. You lie sometimes to make each other feel good. If we told the truth about each other *all* the time, we'd probably be enemies."

Kit and Elaine had been best friends since the fourth grade, so Kit had no fear of their becoming enemies. In fact, they often kidded each other about how they'd be best friends even when they were old and gray. Kit had joked that they could drag-race each other in their wheelchairs.

"Maybe," Elaine said. "But I mean it, about your dancing. You really are terrific. Just like Jennifer Beals in *Flashdance*. Remember how she didn't think she was going to make it, either, against all those other girls?"

"That was just a movie."

"Yeah, but sometimes it happens like that in real life. If you believe in yourself, you can *make* it happen."

Kit smiled at Elaine, warmed by Elaine's confidence in her. "Thanks," she said.

"For what?"

"For being an optimist. And a friend."

"That's me—your friendly neighborhood optimist. I just wish I could feel as optimistic about my own life."

Elaine turned to stare out the window. Kit followed her gaze, watching small shops blend with the huge oaks that sheltered them as the bus rumbled through downtown Glenwood. Kit suddenly felt selfish. She'd been so wrapped up in her own depression over Justin, she hadn't stopped to think that Elaine might be depressed about something, too.

"What's wrong, Elaine?" she asked softly, touching Elaine's arm.

"Oh, it's nothing, really. I'm probably making a mountain out of a molehill. It's just something Carl said when we were out last Saturday night. We were talking about love—how to really know for sure if you're in love with someone. Carl's point was, in order for you to know if it's real, you have to date lots of other people."

"What's wrong with that?"

"Nothing—except that I happen to be his first girl friend. So I guess that must mean he won't know how he feels about me until he's gone out with at least a half dozen other girls."

"He didn't exactly say that," Kit pointed out.

In her opinion, Elaine and Carl were very well matched. Both were Honor Society students, and both had their feet planted firmly on the ground. While they didn't go around school acting gushy and hanging all over each other the way some couples did, it was obvious from watching them together that they really cared about each other.

"You don't know Carl. He's so analytical. Like, he's always conducting these experiments in biology with mice or whatever, to prove a point. He hates jumping to conclusions without a lot of evidence. So what I keep wondering is, maybe it's going to be like that with us. He'll have to experiment with love before he can draw any conclusions about us."

"Love isn't exactly a scientific thing."

Elaine sighed, smoothing her hair. "Try telling that to Carl. He says anyone who wants to be a psychiatrist the way he does has to be a student of human nature, not just in the classroom, either."

They were interrupted by the bus lurching to a stop, followed by a loud hiss as the doors banged open. This was the last bus stop before school. Kit glanced up at the front, where old Mr. Emerson, their driver, sat hunched over the wheel, looking half-asleep. Kit's theory was that Mr. Emerson didn't do anything, it was really the bus that drove itself, like a horse familiar with a certain path.

"Lori . . . back here!" Kit called as she spotted her friend making her way down the aisle.

Lori waved back, breaking into a brilliant smile. *She is so pretty!* Kit thought. Only she didn't begrudge Lori her good looks; her friend was so shy and sensitive she didn't even realize how beautiful she was. Kit was always teasing her about looking like Christie Brinkley, with her long blond hair and cornflower blue eyes. She was also tall and slender like a model, and she had recently admitted to her friends that modeling was something she'd always dreamed of doing. Since then, Lori had already been in two local fashion shows and was waiting to hear from the modeling agencies she'd sent her portfolio to. Kit was sure she'd make it.

Right now, Lori looked as if she'd stepped right out of the pages of some fashion magazine. She was wearing a pair of pin-striped cotton pants the color of daffodils, with a full-sleeved mint-green blouse that had tiny flowers embroidered on the collar. Kit noticed the gold charm bracelet that dangled from her slender wrist as she lifted her arm to wave to someone behind them. On anyone else, a charm bracelet might have looked showy, but on Lori it was just right.

Kit turned and saw red-haired Gayle Rodgers in the second seat beyond theirs. Gayle was a new girl at Glenwood High whom Lori had befriended a few weeks ago. She was very chubby, but Lori was encouraging her to lose weight. Already, according to Lori, Gayle had lost seven pounds. She planned to celebrate when she lost another thirty by going out and buying a new wardrobe, which Lori would help her pick out.

Knowing Lori as well as she did, Kit could understand why her friend wanted to help Gayle. Part of it was Lori's sympathetic nature—she just naturally enjoyed helping people. Also, she herself had once been fat. Kit thought it was amazing that Lori had kept this a secret from her friends for as long as she had, afraid they would think less of her if they knew. Now that her secret was finally out, though, they were all closer than ever, and Kit could see that Lori's confidence had grown now that she no longer felt she had anything to hide.

"Thanks for saving me a seat . . . oops!" Lori shot up again as soon as she'd sat down.

"Sorry," Kit said. "I forgot to warn you about that loose spring. There." She laid her history book over it so Lori could sit down comfortably. "Now you can honestly say you have a place in history."

Lori clapped a hand over her mouth to stifle her giggles. Kit noticed how perfectly shaped each one of her nails was—they were all exactly the same length, painted a pale shell-pink.

"Oh, Kit, you're so funny!"

"I always make jokes when I'm miserable," Kit replied. "At least it's better than crying."

"She and Justin had a fight," Elaine explained.

"Sort of," Kit added. "We didn't exactly fight. It's more what you'd call a cold war."

"Which means," Elaine put in, "that diplomatic relations are still open, but the romance has cooled."

"In other words," Lori said, "you're speaking to each other, but not on kissing terms, right?"

Kit nodded. "Something like that."

Lori put her arm around Kit's shoulders. Kit caught a whiff of some perfume that smelled like violets. Lori's beautiful face was full of sympathy.

"I know how awful you must feel," she said. "Is there anything I can do?"

Kit forced a smile. She didn't want her friends to feel bad on her account. "I don't think there's anything anyone can do. I just wish Justin was as crazy about me as Perry is about you."

A delicate pink blush spread across Lori's cheeks at the mention of her boyfriend. They'd only gotten together a few weeks ago, but they'd been practically inseparable ever since.

"I'm sure Justin cares about you just as much," she said in a soft voice. "You can't compare. It's like saying . . . well, that *Gone With the Wind* was a better movie than *Star Wars*. They're so different."

"Actually, Perry does remind me a little of Clark Gable," Elaine teased. "That dark hair, those sexy eyes . . ."

"Stop right there," Lori commanded, showing some of the spunk she'd developed along with her new confidence. "Anything beyond that is strictly off limits to anyone except me." Her stern words were belied, however, by the smile curling up at the corners of her mouth.

That did it. The three of them dissolved into giggles. When the bus stopped in front of Glenwood High a few minutes later, Kit decided she felt better than she had when she started out, thanks to the support of her friends. Elaine had loaned her a brush and mirror so she could fix her hair, and Lori supplied the lipstick. At least she felt halfway human as she stepped off the bus.

That feeling lasted only a moment. As Kit was crossing the lawn headed for her locker, she caught sight of Justin rounding the corner of the administration building. Her heart seemed to freeze, then it started up again with a powerful rush. Justin looked so handsome! He was wearing his favorite pair of faded jeans and an orange T-shirt, with a Glenwood High sweat shirt tossed over his shoulders, the sleeves knotted casually about his neck. His hair looked more rumpled than usual, his cheeks red with the wind, as if he'd ridden his bike to school.

Kit hesitated. Justin lifted his arm in a stiff little wave, as if he wasn't quite sure how to greet her either. They hadn't seen each other since Sunday, the day they'd spent at the beach. Kit recalled the silent ride home in the back of Danny's truck, and how Justin hadn't even tried to hold her hand, much less kiss her. She knew he thought it was selfish, the way she felt about his summer job, and that only made her angrier. If he would only try, at least, to understand the way she felt, she could forgive him.

Justin was the first to speak. "Hi," he said, stopping a few feet in front of her. Normally, she would've run to him, given him a hug. Today she only stood there, aching inside.

"Hi," she said, so softly she could barely hear

35

herself speak.

"I'm glad I ran into you," he said.

Kit's pulse leaped. What was he trying to say? That he still loved her? That he was sorry?

"You are?" she asked.

"Yeah, I have something for you." He dug into his back pocket, handing something that was curled inside his big fist. Kit saw that it was a silver-and-turquoise earring of hers that had been missing since Sunday. She'd thought she'd lost it at the beach. "I found it in the back of Danny's truck after you got out."

Her heart sank as she took the earring and stuffed it into her purse. "Thanks," she mumbled. "I thought it was lost."

"Don't mention it," Justin replied stiffly. Silence hung between them as they stood there on the lawn, staring at each other. Finally, Justin cleared his throat. "Kit, I . . ."

Just then the bell rang, a deafening noise that drowned out the rest of Justin's words.

"What?" Kit asked.

Justin looked at his watch disconcertedly. He shifted his gaze, staring over at the flagpole which sprouted up from the center of the lawn.

"Uh, nothing," he said. "It was nothing. Forget it." Whatever he'd been about to tell her, he'd obviously changed his mind.

Kit glanced toward her locker. "Well, I guess I'd better be going or I'll be late."

"Me, too."

36

"See you around."

"Yeah, 'bye."

Kit turned away quickly. She didn't want him to see that she was on the verge of tears. Why did he have to act that way . . . as if they were practically strangers? Despite her anger, she'd longed for things to be the way they used to be between them. She'd wanted him to give her that secret smile—the look that belonged to no one but her. She'd wanted to feel his arm slung about her shoulders, casual, but leaving no doubt about where they stood with each other.

Tears stung Kit's eyes in spite of her efforts to swallow them back. Oh, who was she kidding? Maybe Justin didn't love her as much as she'd thought. Maybe he never had. Kit tried to think of something that would cheer her up, something that would keep her from bursting into tears, but her sense of humor seemed to have dried up.

This time, the last laugh was on her.

Chapter Four

"I don't believe it," Kit said.

She stood in the kitchen of the apartment she shared with her mother, the phone glued to her ear. She felt dazed and slightly out of breath, as if she'd just turned a cartwheel.

"Believe it, kiddo," said the voice of Mrs. Rosen. "I have the letter right here in front of me. It's from the head of the scholarship committee. They reviewed your video tape, and they're inviting you to audition for the finals next week."

"I still can't believe it," Kit said again.

Somehow, it just didn't seem real. Hearing her dance teacher tell her she'd been accepted to try out in the finals for a Juilliard scholarship was like watching someone on TV win a new Cadillac. It didn't feel as if this wonderful thing was happening to *her*.

Mrs. Rosen chuckled. "I know. It takes some

getting used to. I remember the first time I got called back on an audition. I was sure they'd made a mistake."

Kit's dance teacher, Roberta Rosen, had been a professional dancer on Broadway before she moved to California. She'd been in a lot of famous shows, like *Guys and Dolls* and *Oklahoma!* Kit loved hearing Mrs. Rosen's stories about theater life. The way Mrs. Rosen told it, Kit could almost feel the excitement of being onstage and hear the thunder of applause. Backstage gossip that was thirty years old intrigued her as if it were yesterday's news.

"Thanks," Kit said breathlessly. "Oh, Mrs. Rosen, thank you so much!"

"Don't thank *me*. You're the one who did it. But don't get too excited yet. You still have the finals to get through."

Suddenly, Kit came crashing down from her dreamlike orbit. "Oh, my God, I just thought of something. How am I going to get there? New York City is so far away!"

"Why don't you talk it over with your parents?" Mrs. Rosen suggested. "I'm sure you can work something out. Tomorrow when you come in for practice, we'll go over the details together."

As soon as she'd hung up, Kit exploded upward in a wild leap of excitement. Her heart was pounding so hard there was a rushing sound in her ears. She forgot all about the can of Diet Pepsi she'd been in the midst of drinking as she whirled around ecstatically.

Kit's mother walked in, balancing a bag of groceries under each arm. She'd just gotten off work, so she was wearing a tailored linen suit and turquoise silk blouse. Kit noticed she was having a little trouble walking in her high heels with the load she was carrying.

"Hey, what's going on? You look like you just won the Irish Sweepstakes." Janice blew a wisp of blond hair out of her eyes as she slid the grocery bags onto the counter.

"Better than that!" Kit cried. She grabbed her mother about the waist, waltzing her across the kitchen. "I did it! I got picked up for the finals!"

Janice threw her arms around Kit, hugging her hard. "Oh, Kit, that's wonderful! I knew it . . . I just knew you'd do it. Wait a minute . . . we have to celebrate."

Janice's face was all lit up, her blue eyes round and suddenly slightly damp. She was like a teenager herself in so many ways, Kit thought. In fact, she looked so young, people often mistook her for Kit's older sister. Janice had the same honey-gold hair as her daughter, though hers wasn't quite as curly, and the same enormous Goldie Hawn eyes. You had to look closely to see the fine lines creasing the corners.

Kit peeked into one of the grocery bags. "What can we celebrate with?"

40

"Oh, forget what's in there," her mother told her. "I was going to throw a pot roast in the oven for dinner. But I've got a better idea now. How does Japanese food sound? There's a new restaurant that opened near work—I hear it's terrific. They have these goldfish . . ."

"They serve goldfish?" Kit interrupted.

"No, silly. The goldfish are in a pool. They're just for decoration."

"Sounds neat." Kit rummaged in the bag, pulling out a carrot. She rinsed it off and bit into it.

"I'll have to call Steve," Janice said, suddenly getting that distracted look she always got when thinking about a boyfriend. Steve was the latest; Janice had been dating him for the last month or so.

"What for?" Kit wanted to know, feeling her happiness deflate. She hated it when her mother tried to wedge one of her boyfriends into their lives.

But Janice didn't even seem to notice. She was too busy fluttering around the kitchen, putting groceries away.

Why couldn't her mother settle down with just one man? Kit wondered in annoyance. None of her friends had a mother like Janice.

Maybe it would be different if Mom weren't so pretty. She seemed to attract men everywhere, even when she wasn't trying—like at the laundromat. Last week, when Kit had gone to pick up some clothes her mother had left in the

41

dryer, she found a note on top of the pile that said: "To the beautiful blond lady—I'm the man who gave you change for two quarters. I'd like to get to know you better. Could we get together for a cup of coffee sometime?" Then he'd given his name and phone number. The last part was what really got to Kit, though. He'd written, "I'll be stuck on spin cycle until I hear from you."

When Janice read the note, she'd only laughed and said, "Well, at least he's got a sense of humor," as if she were used to having strange men leave notes in her dryer.

"I already invited Steve over for dinner tonight," she explained. "I'll just tell him there's been a slight change in plans. He can meet us at Fuji's."

"Mom."

Janice turned to look at Kit. "Yes, honey?" She looked so happy and innocent that suddenly Kit couldn't bear the thought of ruining the moment with the complaint that had been on the tip of her tongue.

"Nothing," she mumbled, taking another bite out of her carrot. A moment ago it had tasted sweet and crunchy; now it was like chewing a mouthful of sawdust.

But Janice must have sensed her sudden switch in mood, for she grabbed Kit's shoulders in a fierce hug.

There were tears in Janice's eyes when she drew back. "You know, in some ways I really envy you. Everything is just beginning for you, Kit. Sometimes I wish I . . ." A wistful expression flitted across her face. "Well, I was going to say I wish I hadn't gotten married so young, but that would sound as if I was sorry I had you. Which I'm most definitely not."

"What would you have done if you hadn't married Dad?"

Janice pulled away with an embarrassed little laugh as she went back to unloading the groceries. "Oh, it all seems so silly now. What I really wanted to be was an actress. But it was just a fantasy. The only thing I ever starred in was my own life. And that role sure wouldn't win me an Academy Award."

Kit smiled. She couldn't stay annoyed at her mother for very long. It was useless to try, for usually, even when Kit was at her angriest, Janice would say or do something so totally disarming that Kit was forced to laugh . . . or to see her mother in a new, sympathetic light.

Kit held her carrot up like a microphone, affecting a nasal announcer's voice. "Here she is, folks—the superstar of the century, a living legend in her own time . . . Janice McCoy!"

Janice picked up on cue, doing a quick shuffle-step on the linoleum in her high heels. It was a game they'd played as long as Kit could remember. Sometimes Kit would pretend to be the announcer; sometimes Janice would. Then the other one would break into an impromptu little dance routine, or start to sing.

But since neither of them could sing very well, it usually ended before it really began—with both of them cracking up.

Kit laughed. "No wonder I've always wanted to be a dancer. I guess it must be in my blood."

"You'll be great at the audition," Janice told her. "I just know it. In fact, I was so sure you'd make it, I mapped out all the arrangements ahead of time."

"You did?"

Stunned, Kit sank down in one of the chairs by the kitchen table. Sometimes, whole weeks went by when Janice was so busy with her boyfriends it seemed as if she didn't know Kit was alive. Then, out of the blue, Janice would do something really fantastic that showed she'd been thinking of her all along.

"Remember that money I was saving for a new sofa? Well, I decided plane tickets to New York would be a lot more exciting. All you can do with a sofa is sit on it."

Kit shook her head, gulping back the tears that had gathered at the back of her throat. "Mom, you're incredible."

"Anyway," Janice rattled on, "we'll save on a hotel, since we'll be staying with your Aunt Miriam."

" 'We?' "

"You didn't think I'd let you go off to New York and leave me home to chew my nails, did you? Anyway, I have some vacation time coming, so it'll work out just perfectly."

44

Kit was so overwhelmed, she didn't have the words to express how she felt. "It seems like such a dream," she finally said, feeling all floaty inside.

She'd never been to New York City, though she'd certainly fantasized often enough about what it would be like. Janice had been there several times to visit her older sister, Miriam, who lived in an apartment overlooking Central Park. The last time Kit had seen her was when Aunt Miriam had flown out to stay with them around the time Janice got divorced. That had been more than three years ago. Kit wondered if her cousin, Ginger, who she still wrote to occasionally, had changed at all from the freckle-faced tomboy she remembered.

Kit handed a soup can to her mother, who was busy stacking them on a shelf in one of the cupboards. "New York is so far away," she added.

She thought about Justin, and how far apart they would be. Then she reminded herself of how far apart they were already. There was a cold feeling in the pit of her stomach, as if she'd swallowed an ice cube.

Janice stopped what she was doing, turning to smile at Kit. "Don't tell me you're feeling homesick already?"

Kit laughed. "Who me—soon-to-be-world-famous dancer Kit McCoy? Not a chance!" But the truth was, she did feel a little scared and nervous. Not just about the upcoming audition, but about her entire future as well.

Janice reached out to smooth a wisp of hair from Kit's forehead. "Growing pains," she stated. "You're thinking about what it's going to be like when you leave home for good."

"I guess that's it." Kit had so many mixed feelings about leaving home. It was going to be especially hard to say good-bye to her family and friends. She thought Christopher Columbus probably felt the same way when he set sail for the New World. He must have been afraid, deep down, that he was wrong, that maybe the world really was flat and he was going to sail right over the edge.

Now, that's how Kit felt—as if she were going to sail right over the edge of the world into a vast unknown void.

Had Justin ever felt this way? she wondered. Probably not. He undoubtedly had his whole life planned out for the next fifty years. Kit couldn't help experiencing a pang at the thought that she wasn't included in it.

"What is it, Kit?" Janice asked, peering at her with a concerned expression.

Kit felt shaky all of a sudden. "Would you mind if we didn't go out tonight? I sort of feel like staying home."

Janice studied her for a moment, her expression puzzled. "What's the matter? Are you feeling okay, honey?"

"I'm okay," Kit told her. "I just don't feel like going out, that's all."

Janice touched Kit's cheek. "I thought you'd want to celebrate. Aren't you happy about all this?"

"I am. I . . . just, well, it's hard to explain. I was just thinking about how pretty soon I'll be leaving home for good and I . . ." She shrugged, unable to fully express the whirlwind of emotions she was feeling.

Slowly, Janice nodded in understanding. Kit relaxed. It was a relief to know her mother understood her need to stick close to home for the moment . . . until she got used to the idea of leaving it for good.

Janice broke into a smile. "You know something? Now that you mention it, I'm not really in the mood for goldfish, either."

Chapter Five

"I'm going to miss you," Lori said, squeezing Kit's hand as they stood at the Pan Am gate, from which Kit's plane would be taking off in a short while.

"Me, too." Alex hugged her so hard, Kit could almost feel her ribs cracking.

"I'll only be gone for ten days," Kit reminded them, fiddling nervously with the strap of her carry-on bag. Her mother was still at the ticket counter, checking in the rest of their luggage. "You guys'll be so busy getting tanned and having fun, you won't even notice I'm gone."

"Until one of us has a crisis and needs to talk to you," Elaine said. "Anyway, what kind of a foursome are we going to make without you? It'll be like driving around in a car with only three wheels."

Kit smiled at the comparison. Elaine's words reminded her of the flat tire they'd gotten driving to the airport in Alex's clunky old car, otherwise known as the "Green Demon." It was a good thing Alex was a whiz at changing tires—as she was at almost everything—or Kit might have missed her plane.

Kit tried not to think about Justin's offer to drive her to the airport. She'd run into him at school a few days ago, and when she told him she was going to New York to audition for Juilliard, he seemed happy for her. He even offered to take her to the airport, but Kit had said no. She was sure he'd only offered out of politeness. Also, she couldn't bear the thought of the hour-long trip to San Francisco International with Justin and her struggling to make conversation. It would be too painful after their former closeness and intimacy.

"You look so sad," observed Lori, ever-sensitive to her friend's moods. "Are you nervous about how you'll do at the tryouts?"

"Sort of," Kit confessed. "I keep imagining they'll have a big gong, like on *The Gong Show*, and halfway through my routine, I'll get gonged."

"That's how I felt before my first fashion show," Lori said. "Remember how nervous I was? I was positive I'd trip walking down the runway."

It was funny that Lori could feel that way when she looked so confident and self-assured. Kit loved the outfit Lori was wearing that day. She had on a baby-blue jump suit with a wide leather sash in a darker shade of purple. A delicately patterned silk scarf was knotted casually about her slender throat.

Kit smoothed her own skirt, suddenly nervous about her appearance. "Do I look okay?" she asked her friends. "I wasn't sure how dressed up the girls in New York are, so I picked out something sort of in between."

The outfit she was wearing actually belonged to Janice—a light cream-colored suit with tiny, almost invisible stripes in pale orange. It had a matching rust-colored blouse, which was slightly too small, since Janice wasn't quite as big in the chest as her daughter, so Kit had left the top two buttons open. Now she worried that her aunt and cousin might think she was trying to look too sexy.

"You look perfect," Elaine reassured her. "Very sophisticated." Quickly, she added, "But not *too* sophisticated." Elaine was wearing a mustard-colored turtleneck tucked into a pair of brown pants.

Alex gave her a devilish wink. "I hear New York is full of gorgeous guys. My cousin Nancy went there last summer, and she met this artist who told her she looked like the Mona Lisa. She showed me his picture, and *he* looked like Robert Redford."

She sat down in one of the orange plastic chairs that lined the lounge area like rows of pumpkins, hooking one brown leg over the other so that her ankle rested on her knee. In her shorts and Indian cotton shirt knotted at the waist, Alex looked comfortably casual.

An image of Justin flashed across Kit's mind. She had a sudden impulse to call him, to say good-bye, but she resisted the urge. What was the point? He was probably too busy to talk to her anyway.

Kit forced a bright smile. "I can't wait to meet my cousin Ginger's boyfriend. She wrote me this long letter about him a couple of months ago. The way she described him, he sounds too good to be true."

"Maybe he isn't," Lori teased. "True, as in faithful, that is."

"Kit will be the guinea pig," Alex said, straight-faced. "If he can resist her, he can resist anyone."

Kit giggled. "Will you guys cut it out? Anyway, I'm not going to New York for romantic reasons. In case you've forgotten, I'm supposed to be trying out for Juilliard."

"That doesn't mean you can't have fun in between the auditions," Elaine pointed out. "Especially since you and Justin . . ." She stopped, catching her lower lip between her teeth. "I'm sorry, Kit, I shouldn't have said anything."

"It's okay," Kit said, staring out the window at a 747 that was taking off as she struggled to bring her emotions under control. "I have a feeling I'm really going to miss him even more than I do now. How much fun can I have if I spend the whole time thinking about someone who's not there?"

At that moment, Janice appeared, clutching their tickets in one hand and a small suitcase in the other. She looked stunning in black velvet jeans and a ruffled Victorian-style blouse, her cheeks flushed with the excitement of the trip and her hair tied loosely at the back of her neck.

Boarding for seats 42 through 22 was announced over the PA system. "That's us," Janice said, glancing at her ticket. She kissed each of Kit's friends on the cheek. "Thanks for bringing us, girls." To Alex she added with a mischievous smile, "And thanks for the lesson in changing a flat tire."

Kit felt strangely choked up as she hugged her friends good-bye. She'd had a flash of what it was going to be like when it *really* did come time for them to say good-bye to each other in a few short months. How was she ever going to manage without them?

"Don't worry, Kit," Lori said in a wobbly voice. "It's only for ten days."

That was Lori for you, Kit thought with a rush of warmth. Lori couldn't stand to see anyone cry. With her, it was like a contagious disease; whenever she saw tears in anyone's eyes, she couldn't keep from crying herself.

"I feel like Dorothy in *The Wizard of Oz* in the scene where she's saying good-bye to her friends," Kit said with a laugh.

The image fit. Elaine, funny and smart, could be the Scarecrow. Ultra-sensitive Lori, who couldn't bear to see anyone hurt, was the Tin Man. And Alex—brash on the outside, tenderhearted on the inside—was the Cowardly Lion.

"You're even wearing your ruby slippers," Elaine laughed, pointing down at the red shoes Kit happened to be wearing.

"Have fun in the Emerald City!" Alex called as Kit made her way to the boarding ramp. Kit blushed as several heads turned to stare at her curiously.

Lori didn't help any by calling out, "Say hello to the Wizard for us!"

Kit giggled in spite of her embarrassment. In some ways, she thought, flying to New York was like visiting a fantasy land. She would be visiting places she'd only dreamed of before; she'd be doing things that she'd done so many times in her imagination, it was going to seem strange when they happened for real. In her mind, as well as in practice, she'd gone over and over the dance routine she'd be doing for the judges, sailing through it perfectly, without missing a beat. Would she blow it in reality? Or even worse, would her best simply not be good enough when she was pitted against some of the most talented kids in the country?

One thing was for certain, though. She might not be going to Oz, but she was going to need all the magic she could get.

Five hours later, Kit's plane landed at the John F. Kennedy Airport following a smooth flight. As Kit and her mother made their way into the crowded terminal, the first person Kit noticed was a tall, willowy girl with curly reddish-brown hair cut very short, and huge slanting green eyes. She was staring at Kit from the other side of the gate, where a mob of people was waiting to greet the disembarking passengers.

The girl looked familiar, but Kit couldn't place where she'd seen her before. On television maybe? She certainly looked as if she could be an actress from the trendy way she was dressed, in a baggy blouse that left one shoulder bare, khaki knickers, and high heels with ankle socks.

Then Kit noticed the short dark-haired woman standing beside the girl, and was struck by a bolt of recognition.

"Miriam!" Janice cried, dashing into the arms of her sister.

Kit continued staring at the girl. "Ginger?"

Ginger gave her a hesitant smile. "Kit . . . I don't believe it's you. Boy, have you changed!"

Kit laughed. "You've grown!"

Ginger's gaze dropped to Kit's chest. "So have you!"

They both laughed.

The last time Kit had seen her cousin, Ginger had been a short, pudgy tomboy with freckles who had worn the same pair of baggy overalls throughout her entire visit. At the time, Ginger was mostly into doing chemistry experiments. She was the only girl Kit had ever known who knew how to make a smoke bomb and concoct invisible ink from scratch.

"Do you still have your chemistry set?" Kit asked.

"Oh, I gave that up ages ago. Here, let me help you with that." Ginger grabbed Kit's shoulder bag, tucking it under her arm as they tagged after Aunt Miriam, who'd stopped chattering with Janice only long enough to give Kit a warm embrace. "I still experiment . . . only it's mostly in the kitchen. I like to make up new recipes for the business."

The business Ginger referred to, Kit knew, was the fancy catering service Aunt Miriam ran. Last year, she'd written to say they were expanding to include a gourmet food shop as well. Kit had been fascinated by the idea; now she couldn't wait to visit the shop.

"I gather from your letters you don't hate boys anymore," Kit said jokingly. She remembered when Ginger had carried around in her back pocket a smudged list of all the boys she couldn't stand.

Ginger shrugged, a little smile playing at her lips. "They're not all bad . . . especially one in particular." A pale blush crept into her cheeks.

"The one you wrote to me about?"

They'd reached the baggage claim area downstairs, but the conveyor belt that brought the luggage out wasn't moving. Ginger and Kit sat down to wait.

"His name is David," Ginger said, getting a dreamy look on her face. "He lives in our building—downstairs, in 3-F. We met when we were walking our dogs one day. His Doberman went after Dixie and our leashes got tangled. Don't you think that's a romantic way to begin a relationship?"

She sighed, leaning forward to prop her elbows against her knees, chin supported by her hands. Suddenly Ginger didn't remind Kit of a sophisticated television star anymore—she looked every bit the love-struck seventeen-year-old. It was probably the first time she'd ever been in love, Kit realized, though personally she didn't see what was so romantic about getting tangled up in dog leashes.

"I can't wait for you to meet him," Ginger gushed. "You won't believe how gorgeous he is. He's six feet two, with chestnut-brown hair, and he's got the most incredible *eyes*. All my friends think he looks like John Travolta. Also, he goes to Horace Mann. Anybody who's *somebody* goes to Horace Mann."

"What's Horace Mann?" Kit asked.

Ginger eyed her incredulously, before bursting into a giggle. "I'm sorry, I keep forgetting. Mom says I do it all the time—I forget that everyone wasn't born in New York. Anyway, Horace Mann is a school."

"Is that where you go?"

"Uh-uh, I go to Stuyvesant. It's public. Mom says there's less chance of me turning into a snob this way."

Looking at her cousin now—her impish grin and sparkly hazel eyes, with those freckles that peeped out despite a carefully applied layer of makeup—Kit didn't think there was much danger of Ginger becoming a snob. She felt relieved. Ginger had looked so sophisticated at first, she hadn't been sure.

"Are you still going with what's-his-name?" Ginger asked. "The guy whose picture you sent me? He was really cute."

"Justin." Even saying his name was hard. Kit's voice caught a little as she did so.

"Uh-oh." Ginger peered at Kit sympathetically. "I think I hit a nerve. Trouble in paradise?"

"Sort of," Kit hedged, not sure how much she wanted to get into it here at the airport, with all these people crowded around. She was tired from the long flight, and that always made her more emotional. She didn't want to make a bad impression on her cousin by bursting into tears. "I guess we're going through what you might call a cooling-off period."

Ginger sighed. "Renee has this theory about relationships. She says they only last so long, then they burn out—like light bulbs. Did you know that Renee's been engaged three times?" Renee was Ginger's older sister; she was twenty-five.

"I heard something like that," Kit said.

She thought about Janice and all the relationships she'd been through. Was it true? Could love only last so long . . . like a fire that burns out after a certain period of time? Maybe the real reason Justin had wanted to work this summer was because he was getting tired of her. . . .

"Mom says she should take insurance on the next one," Ginger said with a little laugh. She looked over at the baggage carousel, which had begun to revolve. "Here comes the luggage. Do you see yours?"

A short while later, with their suitcases installed in the trunk of a battered yellow cab, Kit listened to Aunt Miriam rattle off directions to the driver, who didn't appear to speak any English.

Kit's Aunt Miriam was the kind of person who liked to take charge of everything. No one would guess she and Janice were sisters; they weren't anything alike. They didn't even look alike. Aunt Miriam, who was a few years older, was very petite, almost boyish-looking, with dark hair cut even shorter than Ginger's and blow-dried back at the sides. She didn't look much like Ginger, either, except for her large hazel eyes.

Some people, Kit knew, were misled by Aunt Miriam's size into thinking they could take advantage of her. They usually found out in a hurry that she wasn't the type you could bully or push around.

She remembered one incident in particular that Ginger had written to her about, when Miriam was having an argument with the snooty principal of Ginger's school. During their rather heated debate, he suddenly insisted she call him *Doctor* instead of Mr. Rhinehart, on account of his Ph.D., and Aunt Miriam had replied that would be fine, and, by the way, *she* would prefer it if he addressed her as "Your Majesty."

Kit could easily see why Aunt Miriam's catering business was one of the most successful in the city. She'd started it after Uncle Bill died, and it had been growing steadily ever since. Aunt Miriam ran a kitchen the way a general would run an army.

"I got front-row tickets for the ballet next Thursday," Aunt Miriam announced from the front seat of the cab as it rocketed out into the traffic. "It wasn't easy, but I happen to know the director, who's Russian. I told him I would refuse to fix my special borscht for his next fund raiser if he didn't get me the tickets I wanted. He turned absolutely white!"

Ginger, crammed into the back seat between Kit and Janice, shot Kit a sidelong glance that said, *Do you believe it?*

Janice laughed out loud. "Miriam . . . you haven't changed a bit."

It was dark by the time they reached the outskirts of the city. Kit caught her breath as she stared out the window. Across the river, the Manhattan skyline glittered like a million Christmas tree lights. Kit had never seen anything like it before.

Kit turned to Ginger. "It's fantastic!"

"Wait till you see the view from our apartment," Ginger said. "We're on the top floor. When you stand out on the terrace at night, you can imagine what it's like to fly."

When they got to Ginger's apartment, Kit saw that her cousin was telling the truth. Their apartment was on the sixteenth floor, overlooking Central Park. As Kit stood out on the terrace, a warm breeze ruffling her hair, she felt slightly breathless looking down.

"Don't you ever get dizzy?" she asked Ginger, who sat casually perched on the railing, sipping a Coke.

"Only when I'm out here with David," she said with a wicked smile. "When he's kissing me, I feel as if I'm going to spin right off into orbit. The trouble is"—she lowered her voice, even though it was unlikely that Janice or Miriam, fixing dinner in the kitchen, could hear— "he never wants to stop at kissing."

"I know the feeling," Kit said, remembering how it was before she met Justin. "For a while, I couldn't sit in a boy's car without thinking of it as a battle zone."

"It's not like that with David and me. I mean, I *want* to do more. It's just that I'm not sure I'm ready. It seems like such a gigantic commitment. What if I'm sorry afterwards . . . it'll be too late to turn back. David says that's immature—if two people love each other, nothing should stand in the way."

"The main thing is, you shouldn't feel pressured into doing anything you're not ready for," Kit advised. "When the time is right, you won't have to be talked into it. You'll just *know*."

Ginger was silent as she stared out over the park, which was dark except for an island of light in one corner. In that spot, thousands of tiny pinpoint lights had been strung throughout a grove of trees, outlining each branch. Kit had told Ginger it looked like something out of a fairy tale. In a way it was, Ginger had replied, identifying the area as Tavern on the Green, a famous restaurant where the stars of Broadway often gathered following an opening night.

Finally, Ginger said in a small, embarrassed voice, "Have you . . . well, I know this is kind of personal . . . but have you and Justin, uh, gone all the way?"

Kit hesitated, uncertain of how to respond. If she told Ginger the truth, her cousin might take it as an open encouragement. If she lied, it would inhibit the confidence she could feel growing between them.

Kit decided on the truth. "I didn't want to at first, either," she confessed. "The good thing is, Justin never pressured me. I mean, it was obvious he *wanted* to, but he didn't push me into anything I wasn't ready for. When it happened, well . . . I wasn't really even thinking about it. All I remember is, it seemed right. And it probably wouldn't have if we'd done it any sooner." Kit paused for a moment, then added, "You have to be careful, though, about birth control and all."

"I don't really have too much experience about these things," Ginger said softly. "I know I look a lot older than I am, but I only started dating this year. This"—she held up a lock of her stylishly cropped hair—"was my mother's idea. She decided it was time I had a make-over. The works—hair, clothes, everything. Right after that, I met David. I know he thinks I'm a lot more sophisticated than I really am. He thinks I'm being unfair to *him* by holding out. Like maybe it's some kind of game I'm playing."

Kit had gone out with boys like that before. Their standard line was, "Come on, baby, don't *do* this to me." She hadn't even met Ginger's boyfriend, and already she didn't like him.

"Look at it the other way," Kit said. "If you end up going along with what David wants, just because he wants it, you're being unfair to yourself."

"That's true," Ginger replied thoughtfully. "I know you're right, but when I'm with him it's hard to feel strong. I get so mixed up. And then when he starts in about how I'm *torturing* him

62

. . ." she trailed off, her forehead crinkling in a small frown.

"Next time he says that," Kit suggested, "tell him to take a cold shower."

Ginger laughed as if it were a joke, but Kit had been more than half-serious. Again, she found herself thinking about Justin, how gentle he was, never pushy or demanding. She remembered the times they'd lain together after making love, wrapped in each other's arms, just talking quietly.

A sharp pang cut through her at the realization that she might never have that again with him.

"There's only one thing that can take my mind off romance," Ginger said.

"What's that?"

Ginger threw her head back, inhaling with a loud sniff. "Food! Mom's making her special garlic chicken. It's absolutely out of this world—she made it for the VIP banquet she catered last week, and Mayor Koch himself came up and told her how much he liked it. Come on"—she grabbed Kit's hand—"let's get some before it's all gone. Just don't eat too much, we're trying on clothes at Bloomingdale's tomorrow."

"When do I get time to catch my breath?" Kit asked, smiling again.

Ginger laughed, tossing down the rest of her Coke. "When you're back in Glenwood!"

Chapter Six

". . . and six and seven and *turn* and step, leap, *turn* . . ."

Madame Bouchard stood at the mirror which spanned the length of the rehearsal room, rapping out the rhythm of the dance in her loud, precise voice. Kit could feel those sharp eyes on her as she vaulted up in a butterfly leap.

Kit felt she was dancing well . . . but was it good enough? What she'd seen of the competition so far had left her worried. She glanced out of the corner of her eye at the leotard-clad figures whirling about her, their faces strained with concentration. Most of them would be eliminated by the last leg of the finals. Would she be among those who didn't quite measure up?

The schedule had been presented to her yesterday when she arrived at Juilliard for the first time—two days of general rehearsal under the guidance of Madame Bouchard, head of the school's dance department, and a member of the judging committee, followed by a group audition on Wednesday for the committee, and individual auditions starting Thursday. The group audition was designed to show how quickly each of them could pick up new steps, learn routines, and dance together in a group as chorus members would. The individual auditions, in which they could perform a dance they had choreographed themselves, would spotlight their talents as soloists.

Today was Tuesday, the second day of rehearsals, and Kit was already a bundle of nerves. In Glenwood, she'd been Mrs. Rosen's star pupil. Here she was pitted against star pupils from all over the United States, and even some foreign countries too. Some of her rivals were so good, she might have mistaken them for professionals.

One thought comforted her, though; she'd discovered that they were all anxious and on edge. One girl from Illinois had confided to Kit just a few minutes before in the changing room that she'd been on the verge of throwing up ever since her plane had landed in New York. Somehow, Kit felt better knowing that, even though she sympathized. She was determined to try her hardest and ignore her nervousness.

Kit counted the pace in her head along with Madame Bouchard. *Step, kick . . . contract the ribcage, arch out . . . seven, eight, turn, turn, turn.* She caught a glimpse of herself in the mirror—a flash of limbs in her plum-colored leotard.

She'd tied a red scarf around her hair, and the ends fluttered against her neck as she spun about, fixing her gaze on a small spot on the opposite wall to keep from getting dizzy. She was sweating heavily in spite of the layer of talcum powder she'd dusted over herself before putting on her leotard.

"Now . . . we will practice our leaps. Across the room in groups of two," announced Madame Bouchard. She was a gaunt, elderly woman with dyed black hair that looked like patent leather glued to her head in the shape of a bun. She extended a bony finger toward Kit. "You and you, start first, please."

Kit turned around to see who else Madame Bouchard had pointed to. Her gaze locked for an instant with a pair of eyes so brown that they were almost black, belonging to a dusky-skinned boy with dark, wavy hair.

She'd noticed him before—how could she help it? He was one of the most striking-looking boys she'd ever seen. He looked foreign, which made Kit automatically assume that he was sophisticated. Looking at him, she decided he probably was—sophisticated, that is. There was a hint of amusement in the way his full mouth curled up just the tiniest bit at the corners. The expression in his dark eyes said, "I know I'm good, now I want *them* to know."

He wiped the sweat from his forehead with the back of his muscled forearm. Then he smiled at Kit—his teeth a flash of white against his dusky olive-tinted skin. Together they took their positions at the far end of the room. Kit's knees felt strangely weak as she stared at the long room stretching out before her, empty and waiting. She took a deep breath, knowing that everybody would be watching her, judging her silently.

"Don't look so worried," the boy whispered in a deep, accented voice. "It's only play."

"You mean *practice*," she corrected, thinking, because he was foreign, that he'd gotten his words mixed up.

He smiled again, the smile that quirked up playfully at the edges. His eyes were so dark, they appeared bottomless. Gazing into them, Kit felt herself drawn to him; there was a funny lightness in her stomach, as if she'd just taken a dip on a roller coaster.

"No," he said. "I meant . . . *play*."

He grabbed her hand and squeezed it hard, as if to show her it *was* possible to have a good time . . . even under these circumstances, and that the only *real* reason for dancing was for pleasure.

Suddenly, Kit forgot to be afraid.

When Madame Bouchard clapped her hands, Kit took several running steps and flew into a leap, legs scissoring out, one in front and one in back, as if she were sailing over an invisible hurdle. A sensation of lightness spread through her; she felt as if she were made of air.

She leaped again and again, stretching herself farther, throwing herself a little higher each time. Out of the corner of her eyes, she caught a flash of muscled torso. Her partner wore nothing but a pair of sweat pants. His broad brown chest gleamed with the sweat of his exertion. She glimpsed his expression of happy absorption, and all at once the other people in the room melted away, leaving just the two of them. Kit was aware only of the bronze flash of his body beside hers, and of her own body moving in perfect synchrony. She tossed her head back with her final leap, giving in to the pure joy of the movement.

"Bien!" murmured the dark, exotic stranger, squeezing her hand once more before he stepped away. So he was Spanish! Kit had learned enough Spanish in school to know he was complimenting her.

When the others had executed their leaps, Madame Bouchard announced that it was time to break for lunch; they were to meet again in two hours, she told them.

Kit was making her way to the dressing room when the dark-eyed boy brushed up alongside her and said, "I'll wait for you by the fountain."

68

Just like that! Then he was gone, before Kit had a chance to catch her breath.

"My name is Francisco Villanueva," he said, thrusting out his hand as if they'd just met.

He'd been waiting for her by the big oblong fountain in the middle of the Lincoln Center plaza, exactly as he'd promised. Kit noticed he'd changed into a pair of light blue trousers and white Lacoste shirt. He carried a duffel bag slung over one shoulder. Before she could respond, he added, "And yours is Kit McCoy."

"How did you know?" Kit asked, startled into a self-conscious laugh.

"Simple." He waved his arm in a wide, expressive gesture. "I happen to be very good at reading minds."

Kit felt her face grow warm, remembering how he'd seemed to sense what she was feeling during the rehearsal. Did he know what she was thinking now—that she was wishing he would ask her to have lunch with him? Then she saw by the sparkle in his eyes that he was only teasing her.

"Come on," she giggled. *"Really."*

"Okay . . . I'll tell you." He pointed at the canvas tote bag she was carrying, which had KIT McCOY printed on a piece of adhesive tape stuck to the side.

"Oh," she said, feeling slightly embarrassed as she sank down on the marble ledge surrounding the fountain.

Directly across from her was the high stone-and-glass facade of the Metropolitan Opera House. The sun reflecting off the building's tall windows caused her to squint, despite the sunglasses she was wearing. Everything about New York was so *big* she thought. Big and unbelievably exciting. She hadn't had a moment to be bored or depressed since she'd arrived.

The day before yesterday, Kit and Ginger had gone shopping in Bloomingdale's, where they'd tried on everything from makeup to designer clothes. Kit had heard about Bloomingdale's before, but she was awed by the famous department store, nevertheless. The interior reminded her of some giant labyrinth made of mirrors, and at every elevator there was a beautiful girl passing out free perfume samples. After they left the store, they bought Italian ices in paper cups from a street-corner vendor, and ate them while strolling through the park.

Then last night, Aunt Miriam had taken them all out to dinner at a fancy French restaurant on the Upper East Side. Kit had eaten brook trout stuffed with baby shrimp, which was the best thing she'd ever tasted. The owner had even brought a bottle of complimentary wine to their table, in honor of Aunt Miriam, who was a personal friend.

Yes, ever since she'd arrived in New York, Kit

felt as if she'd stepped into a dream. Francisco Villanueva was like a part of that dream; he seemed too good to be true. At the moment, Glenwood seemed a million miles away.

Francisco was staring at her, his head cocked to one side. "You were perhaps expecting something more dramatic—like this?" He reached out and plucked something from the air behind her ear. "You see, I have many talents besides mind reading."

Kit stared in fascination at the shiny quarter he held out. "How did you do that?"

He shrugged, laughing. "My father taught me that little trick. He's a surgeon . . . but also part gypsy. My grandmother, she was born in a tent. I have inherited my love of travel and adventure from her, I think."

Kit was enthralled. She'd never met a gypsy before. "Where are you from?"

"Madrid. I study dance at the university."

"You speak English very well," Kit observed.

Again, that eloquent shrug, followed by a flash of white teeth against the deep tan of his face. "I travel to many places, so I must learn in order to survive. I speak French and German as well. It's not so hard, if you 'listen' with your eyes. Most people, they only listen to the words. But if you look at someone when they're talking to you, really *look*, you'll see it."

"What?" Kit had barely passed Spanish I. Her knowledge of Spanish had gotten stuck at "*Hola, María. Como está usted?*"

"The meaning behind the words," he said. His dark eyes held hers, as if trying to convey a meaning of their own. Kit shivered. Very formally, he asked, "Will you have lunch with me, Kit?"

She nodded, unable to tear her eyes from his gaze. *This isn't happening . . . it really is a dream*, she told herself as he took her hand and they began walking toward the street.

They rode the subway to Greenwich Village, where they found a café that had tables set out on the sidewalk, overlooking a quaint cobbled street. Francisco ordered wine for them both.

"I'm not supposed to drink," Kit told him, embarrassed. "I'm only seventeen."

Francisco only smiled. "In Europe, we don't concern ourselves so much with age as you Americans do," he said. "Anyway, rules are made to be broken, no?"

"Some rules," Kit agreed with a laugh.

"What counts," he added, "is how you feel. Do you feel as if you are doing something wrong, Kit?"

Kit smiled, feeling confused. He was so different from Justin, who was so straight-arrow he didn't even like to jaywalk if he could help it. She wasn't certain what to make of Francisco.

"No," she finally admitted. "I don't feel as if I'd be doing anything wrong." The truth was, she didn't. Instead, she felt lighthearted, filled with the same sense of abandon he'd infected her with during rehearsal. "But if I expect to dance without tripping over myself when we get back, I'd better not drink anything stronger than 7-Up."

Francisco leaned toward her, brushing the tip of one finger across the back of her hand, which was curled about the stem of her wineglass. Kit shivered, feeling his touch travel through her like an electric shock.

"You're a natural dancer," he told her. "But you have too much fear. It holds you back. Forget the fear and just . . . dance. *Feel* it, don't think it."

"You make it sound so easy! It's not. I feel like I'm under this pressure to, you know, be one of the best. I get so nervous."

"But you *are* the best. It doesn't matter what anyone else says. If *you* feel it, then it's so! Besides"—he shrugged—"it's not really so important, getting into this school or that. Learning comes from many places, not just school. You must know life in order to dance it."

It sounded so poetic when he put it that way, Kit thought. Hadn't she tried to say the same thing to Justin? That you couldn't plan out your whole life before you'd lived it . . . that you had to leave a little room for unpredictability?

The waiter came to take their orders, and Kit, feeling suddenly ravenous, ordered a plate of fettucine. Francisco said he would have a hamburger.

"I like American food," he said. "When I'm in

America, I eat hamburgers and french fries. Someday, when you come to Spain, I'll fix you *my* specialty—paella."

Kit felt tingly at the prospect of going to Spain someday. Why not? she thought. She'd come this far, hadn't she? From now on, the sky was the limit!

Francisco lifted his glass of red wine. "To life!"

"To life!" Kit echoed, feeling very grown-up, even though she was only toasting with a glass of 7-Up.

"Kit." He was staring at her again, that deep, bottomless gaze. "Would you go out with me tonight?"

Kit hesitated. "I don't know if I should. I mean, auditions are tomorrow and I should probably go to bed early . . ." She stopped, suddenly hearing the echo of Justin's voice in her words. She was doing exactly what he had done—putting her future ahead of the present. No, she wasn't going to let herself get stuck in that trap!

"Well?" Francisco was still staring at her, one brow slightly arched.

"On second thought," she said, "I think I will. I mean, why not? It sounds like fun!"

But inside, Kit still wasn't so sure. Deep down, she wondered if maybe . . . just maybe . . . Justin had been right after all to place the future before the present.

Quickly, she banished the thought by taking

a bite of her fettucine. She wasn't going to let anything or anyone ruin the good time she knew she would have tonight if she went out with Francisco—not even Justin.

deal if she had one of the
two ignition keys and all the good time she
knew she would have tonight, if she went out
with Frank Sin—not yet. Austin

Chapter Seven

"He's hard to describe," Kit said as she
strolled alongside Ginger down Park Avenue. It
was late afternoon, and they were walking
Ginger's dachshund, Dixie.

"I can just imagine," Ginger said, "with a
name like Francisco Villanueva. Wow, I'll bet
he's the ultimate in tall, dark, and handsome!"

Today, Kit thought her cousin looked tren-
dier than usual in baggy shorts and a white
tank top with a fishnet overblouse. Purple
running shoes and a pair of mismatched
earrings—one triangular shaped, the other a
plain hoop—completed the outfit. Kit was fascinated by the way New York girls her age
dressed—sort of modified punk. A lot of them
had short hair like Ginger, who wore hers
clipped fairly close in back and at the sides,
with a fluff of curls on top.

In spite of their difference in style, though,

Kit had discovered that she and her cousin had many similar interests. They seemed to love all the same books and movies, and Ginger had a sense of humor that easily matched Kit's own. Also, they both shared the same feelings about going away to college—excited, but a little scared as well.

Kit sighed. "He's sort of like—well, do you remember that part in *An Officer and a Gentleman* when Richard Gere picks up Debra Winger in the end and carries her out of the factory? I know it sounds dumb, but that's how Francisco made me feel. Swept off my feet."

"It *does* sound awfully romantic." Ginger stopped to untangle Dixie's leash, which had gotten wound around a parking meter. "You dip," she scolded affectionately, rumpling the dog's ear. "Why don't you ever look where you're going?"

She straightened, scooping a lock of rusty-brown hair that spiraled down her forehead. Looking at Kit, she said, "I remember that's how I felt with David. It was weird because I'd been thinking about that movie right before I met him. When I saw it, I thought, how unrealistic. Especially that last part. I mean, in real life he probably would have dropped her or something . . ." She smiled dreamily. "Then David came along, and immediately I imagined *him* picking me up like that."

"Too bad life isn't really like the movies," Kit

said ruefully.

Ginger laughed. "Sometimes it is. They could make a movie about you falling in love with a flamenco dancer, for instance."

"He's not a *flamenco* dancer. He just happens to be a dancer who's Spanish."

"Does he speak English?"

"Perfectly. Except he has an accent."

"Oh, I just love men with accents. Whenever I see the Police on MTV, I get goose bumps listening to Sting. But speaking of fantasy, are you sure this guy is for real?"

"He asked me to go out with him tonight," Kit said, adding with a giggle, "And if he doesn't show up, I'll know I imagined the whole thing."

Her cousin paused once again to unravel Dixie, who had gotten herself tangled around a tree trunk this time. Park Avenue was lined with trees, some of them in bloom. Out in the street, the center dividing strip was almost like a garden, bursting with daffodils and tulips. Ginger had told her that spring was the prettiest time of year in New York.

"Are you really going to do it—go out with him, I mean?" Ginger asked as they continued on toward her apartment building.

"Sure. Why not?" Kit tossed back with a lightness she didn't feel.

Ever since she'd impetuously accepted Francisco's invitation, she'd been a little worried. Suppose he discovered how unsophisticated she really was? Also, she still wasn't sure that tonight was such a good night for staying up late, not with auditions tomorrow. Still, if she'd said no, she might have blown her only chance to go out with him. He was so exciting, he probably wouldn't have wanted to waste any more time chasing after a girl who was afraid to live for the moment.

Ginger slid her a curious look. "What about Justin?"

"What about him?" Kit could feel her face growing tight and hot. She didn't want to think about Justin right now, or whether or not she was being disloyal to him. Anyhow, she told herself defiantly, he probably wouldn't care if he knew.

In the same instant, she had a flash of how *she* would feel if she found out Justin had gone out with another girl during her absence. Even the thought of it caused her to feel sick with jealousy.

Oh, why couldn't she get her emotions straight, instead of feeling so mixed up?

"I mean, we're not engaged or anything," Kit was quick to emphasize. "Anyway, Justin is so busy with his career, he probably wouldn't even notice if I was going out with someone else."

"Gosh, that's too bad." Ginger kicked at a leaf that was blowing across the sidewalk. "When you first wrote to me about Justin, you sounded so ecstatic . . . like you'd just landed on the moon."

"I was," Kit answered, feeling sad as she remembered how wonderful it had been . . . right up until the time Justin told her about his summer job. "But I guess in the beginning it's easy to see just what you want to see about a person. It's like those connect-the-dots drawings we used to do when we were kids. You spot a few things you like about a boy, then you fill in the rest—mostly with what you imagine. Sometimes, what you draw doesn't match up with how he really is."

"Yeah, I guess that happens sometimes. I don't really know that much about it, since David is the first boy I've ever been in love with." Ginger suddenly got a bedazzled look. "Oh, Kit, I can't wait for you to meet him! You'll see. He really *is* as wonderful as I described. As soon as he gets back, I'll introduce you." She'd already explained that David was out of town this weekend, visiting his brother up at Harvard; he was supposed to get back sometime today.

Kit smiled. "I'd like that."

They arrived back at Ginger's building just as it was getting dark. Dixie headed straight for the elevator, yapping excitedly and skittering all over the polished marble floor of the lobby. The elevator door opened before Ginger had a chance to push the button.

It was like mental telepathy, Kit thought. A moment ago, they'd been talking about Ginger's boyfriend, then all of a sudden, Ginger cried out, "David!"

She flung herself at the tall, brown-haired boy who stepped out of the elevator. He held a leash attached to a huge, fierce-looking Doberman. With one arm, he scooped Ginger up against him, while attempting to control his dog with the other. Poor Dixie sat trembling on her haunches as David's Doberman strained toward her, a deep growl rumbling from his throat.

"Cook it, Rudy!" David snapped at his dog. Over Ginger's shoulder, he was giving Kit the Look. "Hey, this must be the cousin you've been telling me about."

Kit had been around long enough to know what the Look meant. It was the way a boy stared at you when he was checking you out. She'd been encountering the Look ever since she was old enough to wear a bra. It said: *I don't know you, but I like what I see.* She usually felt uncomfortable when a boy was giving her the Look, especially when that person happened to be her cousin's boyfriend.

Ginger, of course, was so happy to see David, she didn't notice a thing.

"David, this is Kit," she bubbled, beaming up at him adoringly.

Well, at least he was as handsome as Ginger had described, Kit thought. He had the kind of face, though, that was almost *too* perfect. Kit took inventory: dark-brown hair, perfectly styled and blow-dried to perfection, green eyes that radiated confidence, and a chin like John Travolta's with a deep cleft. He wore a navy blue blazer with a checked shirt and skinny tie. John Travolta gone preppie.

"Hi, Kit!" He was giving her the complete treatment—the full-on smile that went along with the Look. "Boy, you California girls. With a tan like that, you must spend a lot of time at the beach."

Kit translated, *I'll bet you look great in a bikini.*

Kit shrugged. "Not too often. I work after school, so I'm pretty busy."

"Kit's a dancer," Ginger reminded him. "She's trying out for Juilliard."

"Right—you told me." To Kit, he said, "Dancing happens to be one of my favorite things. Right up there in my life. I saw *Flashdance* three times, not counting video."

Kit glanced over at the Doberman, which had stopped growling at Dixie and was pacing nervously about at the end of his leash. "Hey, your dog is . . ." But David was too busy staring at her to notice what was happening.

Before Kit could warn him, Rudy the Doberman had cocked his leg against the potted palm tree which stood in a huge stone urn by the elevator. David frowned in annoyance, jerking hard on the leash. When he could see it was too late, though, he merely shrugged.

"I guess I'd better be going," he laughed.

"Rudy's the impatient type." He kissed Ginger lightly on the mouth. "Later." Then he turned to Kit. "Nice to meet you. We'll all have to get together some night . . . maybe go dancing."

"Isn't he wonderful?" Ginger slumped against the inside of the elevator as soon as the door had slid shut. Her eyes were half-closed, and she wore a lovesick expression.

Kit thought about the puddle on the floor of the lobby, which some poor janitor would be stuck cleaning up. "Uh, yeah . . . he seemed really nice."

Ginger went on chattering about David, even after they'd reached the sixteenth floor and let themselves into the apartment, but Kit only half listened. David-this and David-that: the time Ginger's mother catered a party David's parents had thrown, and Ginger and David had sneaked off in the middle of it; the night, after David's prom, when they watched the sunrise from the deck of the Staten Island ferry; the night they were alone in her apartment, when they almost . . .

Kit was jolted to full attention.

"We had our clothes off and everything," Ginger was saying. She sat on her bedspread, a giant silk-screen blowup of a Doonesbury cartoon, staring at the artsy neon sign on the opposite wall, which spelled out "Ginger." "We almost went all the way that time, only . . . I don't know, I just *couldn't*. I felt like I was standing on the edge of this cliff and . . . ."

83

"Don't." Kit gripped Ginger's freckled arm. Ginger stared at her. "Don't what?"

"Don't jump," Kit warned with sudden vehemence. "Don't jump off that cliff. Not until you're absolutely sure." She felt certain that Ginger would be making a huge mistake if she went all the way with David.

Kit couldn't bring herself to tell Ginger why, though. It was just this instinct she had about David. But suppose she was wrong? Well, she knew what it was like to become disillusioned about your boyfriend, and she didn't want Ginger to be hurt in the same way.

"But *you* did," Ginger pointed out. "Are you sorry?"

Kit thought about it. She remembered so clearly what it had been like, the tender way Justin had held her and kissed her, never forcing her, waiting for her to make the final decision. And afterwards, when she was feeling strangely emotional and had burst into tears, Justin had comforted her. He'd seemed to understand that she wasn't crying because she felt she'd done something wrong—only because she felt so fragile and somehow changed.

Kit shook her head slowly. "No," she said. "I guess I'm not."

Kit was more confused than ever. If it was over between her and Justin, why did she still feel this way about him?

"There is a sadness in you." Francisco was

gazing deep into her eyes. "I feel it . . . even when you are smiling."

"It's nothing," Kit said. "I guess I'm just a little homesick."

They were dancing to a slow number. Kit had her arms around his neck, looking up at him. Francisco wasn't like other boys she'd danced with before. He didn't press up against her, as if he were trying to grind himself into her. In fact, he held her so lightly she was barely aware of it. But, oh, the way he moved! Slowly, seductively, he guided her across the crowded dance floor, never missing a beat, his dark eyes fixed on her face. With a flick of a shoulder, a liquid twist of his hips, he conveyed more sexuality than all the sweaty-palmed boys she'd ever known. It was almost frightening—like having him make love to her, only she couldn't accuse him of doing anything wrong.

He was wearing a light-colored raw silk suit and dark red tie, only he'd loosened the tie and opened the top buttons of his shirt. It was hot, and they were both perspiring a little. Francisco's rumpled dark hair seemed to glisten in the semi-darkness. The flashing strobes of the disco were reflected in his black eyes.

Kit licked her lips, which suddenly felt very dry. She was glad they were not alone, or there was no telling what would happen. She wasn't sure she would be able to resist the powerful effect he had on her.

It had been like this ever since he picked her

up. First, they'd eaten dinner at a fun Italian restaurant, where the pizza was baked over charcoals and the waiters all took turns getting up on a little stage and singing. At one point, Francisco had even sung along with one of the waiters in a surprisingly good baritone. Kit had felt proud when several people applauded their table. It was the kind of impetuous thing she couldn't imagine Justin . . . or herself . . . ever doing.

Afterwards, he'd brought her here, to a disco called The West End Express. It was crowded, mostly with kids around their age. The centerpiece of the room was an old trolley car which had been cleverly converted into a bar. There were lots of flashing colored lights and mirrors, too, which, combined with the wine she'd drunk at dinner and the hypnotic effect Francisco had on her, were making Kit feel sort of dizzy.

"Would you mind if we sat this next one out?" she asked when the song they were dancing to ended. "I guess all that rehearsing today tired me out more than I realized."

"I have a better idea," Francisco said, curving an arm lightly about her waist as they made their way off the dance floor. "It's a warm night. We'll do as all lovers in New York do . . ."

Kit shivered, her face growing even hotter than it already was. "Lovers"? What was he suggesting? "Uh . . . I don't know what you mean."

He smiled, as if she'd been silly to ask. Wasn't it obvious? "We'll ride through the park in a horse-drawn carriage," he said.

"Oh." Kit smiled back. "That sounds like fun." She'd seen those funny old-fashioned carriages around the city; Ginger disdained such things as "touristy," but Kit figured, since she was a tourist, why not?

Outside, they walked a short way over to the entrance of the park, where several carriages stood waiting. Francisco looked at them all before choosing the nicest one—a gleaming black carriage with gold stenciling on the sides pulled by an enormous dappled-gray horse. After he'd paid the driver, he helped Kit up onto the cushioned wine velvet seat. Kit sank back with a shiver of delight. It was so luxurious! There were even bud vases with flowers in them attached to the sides.

"It feels so elegant!" she cried, glad she'd worn one of her best dresses. It was simple but dressy—a white summer shift of filmy cotton voile with a lilac sash that tied loosely about her hips.

"Shall I ask the driver to take us to your palace, Princess?" Francisco teased, his dark eyes full of dancing lights.

"Oh, Francisco," she giggled.

"What's wrong?" he asked as he hoisted

himself up beside her in one easy, graceful movement. "You think I am joking? You *are* a princess if you wish to be. Tonight, anything is possible."

"No, I'm not," Kit protested. "I'm just a girl from California."

Francisco looked stricken, as if he were deeply disappointed in her. "You must have magic . . . or you have nothing. Excuse me"— he shook his head—"my English sometimes fails me. I meant to say, you must have imagination."

"I liked it better the other way," Kit said, reflecting on what he'd said. "Magic. You're right. I guess we all could use a little more magic."

The carriage started up the drive at a leisurely pace. Leaning back against the seat, Kit gazed up at the stars winking through the dark canopy of trees overhead. Francisco was right. If people didn't leave room for magic in their lives, things would get pretty dull.

Francisco leaned close, his arm encircling her shoulders. Kit caught the musky scent of his after-shave. "Your family interests me," he said.

Kit laughed. "You mean my mother?" She had noticed when Francisco came to pick her up that he and Janice seemed to hit it off right away. While Kit finished getting dressed, she'd listened to Janice entertaining him out in the living room with funny stories of the time she'd gone to Spain when she was in college.

Francisco nodded. "She is a dreamer like you, I think."

"A little too much, sometimes," Kit agreed. "She tends to be sort of flighty—especially where men are concerned."

"You disapprove?"

"Well, sometimes I wish . . . well, I wish she would stay in one place more—like home."

"Then she would be ordinary. Predictable." Francisco was frowning again. "For a lover of life to be predictable is to be . . . dead."

"I suppose so." Kit stared at him, mesmerized.

Francisco touched her hair. "You're very special, Kit." His voice was husky. "Also, very beautiful."

Kit grew warm all over as Francisco cupped her chin in his hand, and brought her face to meet his. Once again, she had the feeling that this wasn't really happening . . . that it was something out of a dream. She closed her eyes and felt his mouth against hers. He was so passionate!

Despite her growing excitement, she felt a little afraid. Francisco seemed so . . . experienced. He'd probably kissed hundreds of girls. He was a couple of years older than she— nineteen, he'd told her—so he probably expected more. Suppose he expected her to go all the way? Even if she *had* done It with Justin, that didn't mean she would jump into bed with just anyone.

Francisco continued kissing her, but he didn't try anything else. Kit relaxed. She felt as if she were being pulled underwater by a warm, insistent current.

Francisco kissed the way he danced—with more suggestion than power. The way he ran his tongue gently across her lower lip . . . exploring her . . . it was more intimate in some ways than if he'd undressed her. His intensity was overpowering.

Kit was the first to pull back. She felt breathless, as if she would have drowned if she hadn't come up for air. Francisco didn't seem annoyed when she resisted his next attempt to kiss her. She was surprised that he didn't persist. Kit was used to boys, not including Justin, who wouldn't take no for an answer.

"Are you angry with me?" she asked in a small voice, when several more minutes passed without his trying anything.

Francisco turned to her with a smile. "Should I be?"

"No . . . I was just wondering. You seemed so . . . quiet."

"Are you afraid I'm angry because you wanted to stop kissing?" He chuckled softly. "I'm sorry to disappoint you."

Kit was so flustered she could barely speak. "I didn't mean you *should* be angry," she stammered. "I meant . . ."

"I know." He smoothed the hair back from

her face. His eyes were black pools in the darkness. Kit was lulled by the hollow clocking sound of the horse's hooves against the cobbled street. "You're used to boys who want too much . . . before you're ready to give. There are some things I don't believe in rushing."

"Do you have a girl friend?" Kit blurted out.

"I make no promises . . . to anyone." Then he added with a quick smile, "But I believe in love most definitely!"

Kit sighed. "Sometimes, I don't know. I mean, maybe love is just one of those things that doesn't last, no matter how much you want it to."

"You expect too much, Kit. If you try to possess love, it will die—like a butterfly in captivity. You must take it as it comes . . . then, when it is ready to fly away, you won't be sad."

"Have you ever been in love?" Kit asked. "I mean, *really* in love?"

Francisco kissed her again on the lips, gently. "Tonight, I am in love. Maybe tomorrow, too." He shrugged. "Who knows?"

Kit allowed him to kiss her again, this time more deeply. Francisco was right. She wasn't going to let herself think about the future . . . or even the past. She was just going to enjoy this moment while it lasted.

"I've never been in anyone's hotel room before," Kit said, feeling more nervous than she had in her entire life. What she meant was,

91

she'd never been in a boy's hotel room before.

She couldn't believe she'd allowed Francisco to convince her to come here. Well, he hadn't actually *convinced* her, not with words, anyway. Her only excuse was, she'd been in a semi-trance when he invited her, unable to say either yes or no.

He'd taken her silence as yes, and had asked the cab driver to let them off at his hotel.

Kit looked around her. It was a plain room, nothing too fancy. The most prominent thing about it was the bed—it sort of stared her right in the face the minute she walked through the door.

Francisco seemed to sense her nervousness. In the semi-darkness, he put his arms around her and kissed her. "There is nothing to be afraid of, Kit," he murmured, his lips against her hair. "Come. Lie down with me. I want to hold you."

Kit allowed herself to be led over to the bed, which was unmade. But she wouldn't lie down; she only sat on the edge. *This is crazy!* she told herself. Every time she closed her eyes, she saw Justin's face. She felt rooted to the spot, so stiff and wooden that she couldn't seem to uncross her legs, even when Francisco rubbed his hand over her kneecap, gently working his fingers around the side to pry her clamped knees apart.

The funny thing was, in a strange way she *wanted* to make love with Francisco. She believed everything he'd told her, about living life for the thrill of the moment. Yet something was holding her back. . . .

"Francisco, I . . ." she started to say.

He placed a finger against her lips. "Hush. Words will only spoil it. You must say it with your body . . . as in dancing."

"But . . ."

This time he smothered her protest with a deep, searching kiss. Slowly, inexorably, Kit felt herself being lowered backwards onto the bed. She was powerless to resist. Francisco wasn't forcing her; it was more like being hypnotized. She was aware of everything—the tangled sheets pressing into her back, Francisco's gentle, but insistent hand on her thigh—but it was also as if she were in a trance.

"Your skin is so soft—like the wings of a butterfly," Francisco murmured, stroking higher on her leg.

If anyone else had said something as corny as that to her, Kit would have laughed . . . but coming from Francisco in his husky accented voice, it sounded just right. As in a dream, where everything that's happening makes perfect sense, but when you wake up the meaning fades away and it's all a jumble. Would all this be a jumble to her when she looked back on it tomorrow?

Francisco went on murmuring poetic endearments while he kissed her some more. He didn't confine himself to kissing her mouth, either. He kissed her whole face. A warm tingle raced through Kit as his lips brushed over her eyelids. A moment later, he was nibbling on her ear and nipping her gently on the neck.

Suddenly, her dress fell open in back. Somehow, while kissing her, he'd managed to work her zipper free. Kit began to tremble. How had *that* happened? Usually, the Zipper Olympics, as she called it, started out with the boy pleading with her . . . and ended up with an all-out tug of war. With Francisco, zippers seemed to open magically at his touch—including his own, she noticed with a shock.

Now, he was unbuttoning his shirt. His muscular dusky-skinned chest gleamed softly in the dim light coming from a single lamp he'd left on by the bed. His black eyes were fixed on her with an intensity that was almost frightening. A coil of hair dipped over one eyebrow, adding to the Bedroom Look.

"*Te amo*, Kit," he whispered as he lowered his half-naked form so that he was practically lying on top of her. He began kissing her neck again. Kit shivered with a sensation that was half fear, half delight. *Te amo*, she knew from her faltering Spanish, meant *I love you*.

Suddenly, Kit realized what was wrong. She didn't love *him*. He was handsome and exciting, and she liked him a lot, but she didn't *love* him. No matter what, she couldn't do It with a boy she didn't love. It would be . . . well, *wrong*.

Gently, Kit disentangled herself from Francisco's embrace. She sat up. No longer a blob of jelly, she felt herself harden with her resolve.

"I'm sorry, Francisco," she said. "I . . . I'm just not ready for this. I like you a lot, but . . . I don't love you."

Francisco frowned slightly, though he seemed more confused than annoyed. "Love," he said. "You expect too much. Let it fly! If you love only for one night, it is enough, no?"

Kit shook her head. "No . . . not for me. I guess I'm just not ready to fly. Anyway," she said in a feeble attempt to lighten the situation by making a joke, "I'm not wearing my crash helmet."

Judging from her past experiences with boys, Justin aside, Kit half-expected Francisco to get angry. But he didn't. He only gave one of his mysterious shrugs.

"If that's how you feel, then you must go," he said. Francisco rose, zipping his pants back up, but not bothering to button his shirt. Lounging against the door frame in the half light with his shirt open, he reminded Kit of a sexy poster she'd once seen of Erik Estrada.

Kit knew she had to get out fast—before she fell under his spell again.

She managed to get herself zipped up in back. Then she hunted for her shoes, which had gotten kicked off at some point. She found one of them tangled among the sheets. The other one was under the bed. As she was slipping it on, she happened to glance at the clock on the nightstand. One A.M.! She hadn't realized it was so late. Oh my God, she had to get back! Her mother and Aunt Miriam would be frantic. Worried about Kit being alone in a strange city with a strange boy, Janice had made her promise to be back by twelve.

"Good-bye, Francisco!" she cried in an embarrassed rush, not knowing what else to say, as she was hurrying out. Kit felt panicked at the prospect of trying to hail a cab on her own, but she didn't know how to ask Francisco to help her, after the way things had turned out.

Kit hadn't gone more than a few steps when she felt Francisco's hand against her arm. She froze.

"Wait," he said. "I'll go with you." When he saw her surprised look, he smiled and said teasingly, "When you don't fly, you must take taxis . . . which aren't always so easy to find at night."

Chapter Eight

Kit took a deep breath. In her head, she counted. *One . . . two . . . three . . . four . . .*

"I always get the hiccups when something is really bugging me," Ginger said over her shoulder. "My therapist says it has to do with keeping my feelings to myself." Ginger had been seeing a therapist ever since her father died, though she'd confided to Kit that she didn't really think she needed to—it was just that her mother was sure she'd turn out to have some horrible problem with men later on in life if she didn't.

They were standing in the enormous kitchen of Ginger's apartment. Kit was helping Ginger fill a tray of tiny cream puff shells with custard squeezed from a pastry tube. Aunt Miriam was catering a fancy party in SoHo, and she needed eight dozen miniature eclairs by tonight.

Kit let her breath out when she'd finished counting up to ten. She waited for a moment, on guard against the next attack of hiccups. When it didn't come, she allowed herself to relax.

"I wonder what your therapist would say about a girl who couldn't make up her mind between spending an exciting summer in Europe . . . or a boring one at home," Kit said glumly.

"It all depends." Ginger licked a blob of custard from her finger. "A summer in Europe with Francisco sounds fantastic, all right. Mom and I spent one August in Europe once. You can't imagine how fabulous it is. All these beautiful old buildings and, oh, you'd just *die* if you saw Paris! I'll bet it's the most romantic city in the world. Just think of it—a moonlit stroll along the Champs-Élysées with Francisco, sipping espresso in a sidewalk café." She closed her eyes, a dreamy expression floating across her impish features. No doubt she was imagining what it would be like with David. Suddenly her eyelids flew open, and her forehead creased in a tiny frown of uncertainty. "But on the other hand, if you're still in love with Justin . . ."

"Even if I *did* love Justin, which I'm not sure I do, what good would it do if he doesn't love me?" Kit replied stubbornly.

Kit had been in a state of confusion since yesterday, when out of the blue Francisco had invited her, as casually as if he were suggesting a date to the movies, to go with him on a backpacking trip around Europe that summer.

They'd been walking to the subway together following Wednesday's group audition when he suggested it. Kit had been feeling bad about her performance. She'd been tired from her date with Francisco the night before, so her dancing, she thought, had been limp and lifeless.

"Don't worry so much—you danced like an angel," Francisco had reassured her, putting an arm about her. Then, right there in front of the subway turnstile, he kissed her. "But you still have much to learn about life before you can be truly alive when you dance. Come with me this summer, Kit. You would love Europe . . ."

Kit felt as if she'd been caught up in a cyclone. Now, a day later, her head was still spinning. Should she play it safe—stay home this summer and hope that Justin would be able to spare five minutes for her here and there? Or should she take a chance on love and life with Francisco in Europe?

Live for the moment.

Or die of boredom for the summer.

"How can you be so sure Justin doesn't love you?" Ginger asked. They'd finished one tray and were starting on another. Kit refilled her pastry tube from the big pot on the sink. "I think you ought to talk to him before you make up your mind. Give him a chance. Maybe he really misses you."

"It would serve him right if he does," Kit said. She squeezed too hard, and a huge blob of custard squirted out. She cleaned it up and started over.

"Anyway, missing a person when they're gone doesn't count. It's how you act when they're *there*."

"You could call him," Ginger suggested. She shot Kit an impish grin. "You know what they say—'reach out and touch someone.' "

"Give me a break!" Kit giggled, brandishing her tube at her cousin in mock threat.

"I'm serious," Ginger said, swallowing back her own giggles. "You should talk to him, Kit. My therapist says you have to confront whatever is bothering you. Most people think it'll just go away if they ignore it, but usually the problem only gets worse."

Kit remembered the time she'd had a pregnancy scare. Not wanting to confront such a terrible problem, she tried ignoring it instead. But she'd ended up making herself sick with worry and had driven her friends and Justin up the wall as well.

Maybe Ginger was right. Maybe she should call Justin. In her heart, she still loved him—in spite of believing that he didn't love her anymore.

"He went to visit his grandparents for a few days," Kit mused aloud. "Maybe it wouldn't hurt to call . . . just to make sure he got back all right."

Ginger grinned. "You can use the phone in my bedroom—that way you'll have more privacy. Mom calls it the 'hotline,' because I spend so much time gabbing with David."

"In that case," Kit said on her way out of the kitchen, "I promise not to tie it up for too long."

There was a tight knot of apprehension in Kit's stomach as she picked up the phone in Ginger's bedroom. She realized she missed Justin a lot more than she wanted to admit. Her fingers were trembling as she dialed the area code for Glenwood followed by Justin's number.

It rang several times before someone picked it up.

It was Justin's father.

"Hi, Mr. Kennerly. It's Kit. Is . . . is Justin there?"

"Just a minute, Kit, I'll see." There was a hollow-sounding clunk as he put the receiver down. Kit could see it in her mind as clearly as if she were there—the white phone sitting on the little red enameled table in the hallway, Justin running to snatch it up . . .

But the phone remained silent for what

seemed an eternity. Obviously, Justin wasn't running to get it. Kit began to feel panicky. What if he didn't want to talk to her? Then again, if he got on the phone, what was she going to say? She realized she hadn't planned this out very well; she hadn't wanted to give herself time to think about what she was doing or she might have chickened out.

Just as Kit was about to hang up, Justin's voice came over the line. "Kit . . . is that really you?"

"It's me." Kit felt her voice shrinking, along with her confidence.

"You sound different. Maybe because it's long distance. You're still in New York, aren't you?"

"Mmm. You sound different, too." She swallowed. The knot in her stomach had moved up into her throat. "Did you have fun at your grandparents'?"

"Yeah, it was great. One of my cousins threw a big party for me. The day before I left, we all went canoeing down the Russian River. It was wild. Our boat tipped over and we all got drenched. Melinda lost one of her sneakers . . ."

"Sounds like fun," Kit said, trying to keep her voice light. Inside she was dying. Justin was treating her as if she were a buddy who'd called up for a friendly chat. It was obvious, too, that he'd been having a good time without her, that he didn't miss her a bit. And *who* was Melinda?

"How's New York?" Justin asked. "Have you visited King Kong yet?"

"Huh?"

"The Empire State Building."

"Oh, that. Not yet."

"Hey, how are the tryouts going?"

"Pretty good. I'm doing my solo routine for the committee tomorrow."

"Well . . . good luck. You probably won't need it, but good luck anyway."

"Thanks."

Suddenly, Kit couldn't remember why she'd called, or what she'd wanted to say. She bit her lip to keep from crying. This wasn't turning out at all the way she'd hoped. Justin sounded so stiff. If he still loved her, why was he acting as if they were just casual friends, nothing more?

Anyway, there was no point in asking him if he still loved her. The answer was obvious, wasn't it? He didn't at all.

After a long empty silence, Justin said, "Kit . . . was there something you wanted to ask me?"

"What do you mean?"

"Well, I was just wondering if maybe there was some special reason you called."

Kit couldn't bring herself to tell him the truth. She was certain it would only mean

103

being further humiliated. Suddenly, she was sorry she'd called. Justin was the one who should be calling *her*. After the way he'd ruined their plans for the summer, *he* should be the one worrying about their relationship.

"No special reason," Kit said in a tight voice. The lump in her throat had turned to an ache. "I wasn't doing much, so I just called to see how you were."

"Oh, I see."

Kit took a deep breath, closing her eyes. "Well, I guess I'd better be going. I'm supposed to be helping Ginger."

"Yeah, I've gotta go, too. I'm meeting someone in a few minutes."

A girl? Kit wondered with a stab of jealousy. But she didn't ask. "Well, 'bye," she said. "I guess I'll see you when I get back."

"Sure. Good luck with the auditions and everything."

As soon as she hung up, Kit felt it—a bubble rising in her throat. When it reached the top, it exploded. Her whole body jerked in a loud hiccup.

Kit collapsed on the bed, feeling more miserable than ever. She couldn't give in to a good cry now. It was pathetic. Who ever heard of a broken heart with hiccups?

"Skating in Central Park? I don't know . . . I haven't roller-skated since I was a little kid!"

Kit stared at Francisco, lounging in the front

doorway with two pairs of roller skates, tied by their laces, dangling over his shoulder. When he'd told her to wear something casual for their date Thursday afternoon, she'd never expected *this*.

Francisco grinned. "All the more reason you should. To be entirely grown up is a great tragedy."

"Is it safe? I mean, what about all that stuff you read in the newspapers about people getting mugged in the park?"

"I have no fear," he laughed. "Besides, for someone to catch us, he would have to be wearing roller skates, too."

Kit's resistance melted as he leaned forward, brushing his lips against hers. Francisco was so crazy . . . so unpredictable. . . .

She laughed. "Oh, what the heck. Why not?"

A dose of the unpredictable was exactly what she needed right now to dispel her depression over Justin.

"What's this I hear about roller-skating?" Janice popped up off the couch as Francisco sauntered into the living room. She wore a look of bright curiosity.

Janice had just taken a shower and was dressed in a long blue kimono that matched her eyes. Her hair was still quite damp and had dripped down the front, forming dark wet patches on the pale blue silk. Kit was slightly embarrassed. Her mother had known Francisco was coming over—why couldn't she have put something decent on? Why did she have to always go around looking so . . . well, so unlike anyone's mother?

"With your permission, I'm taking your daughter roller-skating," Francisco explained. "I promise I will let no harm come to her, Mrs. McCoy."

"Call me Janice, please," Kit's mother told him, smiling. "I feel so old when people call me 'Mrs.'! Anyway, I'm not married, so it doesn't really apply."

Did she have to advertise it? Kit wondered in exasperation. Why couldn't Janice act her own age, instead of pretending to be Kit's?

Francisco shrugged. "Age. It's of no importance. I believe one is only as old as one wishes to be."

"Right now, I wish I were seventeen," Janice sighed wistfully, not seeing the look of dismay Kit shot her. "I used to love to go roller-skating when I was a teenager—especially down steep hills. Oh, I was so crazy in those days!"

"You must come with us, then!" Francisco offered impulsively. "There is enough space for all of us."

Kit groaned inwardly. Francisco was only being polite because he didn't want Janice to feel left out. But Kit couldn't help admiring his generosity toward Janice even while she fought her rising annoyance.

"Mom was just kidding," Kit said lightly, attempting to make a joke of the whole thing.

"Besides, you only brought two pairs of roller skates."

Unfortunately, Ginger happened to walk in at exactly that moment. She'd been running around the apartment in a frenzy, getting ready for her date with David. She paused halfway across the living room, looking distracted. She was wearing one sneaker while she carried the other. In a pair of striped Oshkosh overalls and a bright yellow T-shirt, she looked more like the Ginger Kit had remembered as a child.

"You need an extra pair of roller skates?" she asked Janice. "I have some in my closet that would probably fit you. We have the same size feet, Aunt Janice. I know, because I tried on a pair of your shoes one time."

Janice glanced uncertainly at Kit. "Well, I don't want to intrude. After all, it's your date. . . ."

She looked so disappointed, Kit couldn't bear it. It was a real problem, she thought. She could never stay annoyed at her mother for more than five minutes at a time. Sometimes, Kit felt sort of responsible for her mom's happiness, as if *she* were the mother and Janice the daughter.

"Why don't you come, Mom?" Kit said with a forced cheeriness. "I don't mind."

"Are you sure, honey?"

"Sure I'm sure."

Janice beamed at Kit. "I'll go change," she

said, hurrying off in a flutter of blue silk. "I'll only be a sec!"

Francisco slipped an arm about Kit when they were alone, nuzzling her hair. He was wearing tight-fitting jeans and a navy sweat shirt that showed off the compact muscularity of his arms.

There was a strange lightness in the pit of Kit's stomach as she gazed up into those dark eyes full of mystery. She felt a little dizzy, too. It was like being in a high place and looking down, afraid you were going to fall.

But why should she be afraid? Francisco wasn't just exciting, he was also good-hearted. Look at the way he'd been so quick to include Janice in their plans.

Suddenly, Kit knew what her answer was going to be to Francisco's invitation for the summer. If she could convince Janice to let her go, she was going to say yes. Money wasn't a real problem, since Kit's father had offered to buy her a used car for graduation. She could probably get him to give her the money instead.

One thing was for sure, Kit decided—she didn't have to worry about Justin missing her. He would probably be relieved to have her out of the way!

But for some reason—Kit wasn't sure exactly why—she couldn't bring herself to be happy about her decision.

Chapter Nine

Kit was so nervous, she was sure her knees would collapse if she stood up. She sat stiffly on the edge of her folding chair, which was one of several dozen that had been set up around the perimeter of the studio. The judges occupied a long table at the front of the room. She was watching Kirsten Kruger, the girl from Germany, dance to the theme from *Superman*. Kit's turn to audition was next. Only how on earth would she be able to perform out there in front of all those people?

She concentrated on Kirsten, hoping it would take her mind off what lay ahead. Kirsten's was a bouncy, stylish routine with lots of gymnastic moves.

While it was difficult to tell from the impassive expressions on the judges' faces whether or not they liked her, Kit caught sight of one judge smiling as he wrote something down.

109

Kirsten's good, Kit thought, they *must* be impressed!

When it was over, a number of people applauded. Kit clapped, too. She was happy for Kirsten, but at the same time, she couldn't help feeling dismayed. Most of the other kids were so good. She was afraid she wouldn't measure up next to them.

If only Francisco were here! But he wasn't scheduled to perform his routine until tomorrow, the last day of tryouts. Kit wished he'd come anyway. Right now she could really use his breezy encouragement and cocksure grin.

She thought about their date on Thursday when they'd gone roller skating in Central Park. It was a day Kit was sure she'd remember for the rest of her life—clear, sunny, perfect . . . perfectly unpredictable, that is.

The three of them had skated all over the park, racing each other in places where the path was wide enough. Then Janice decided to show off her once-famous stunt, and she charged downhill . . . straight into a duck pond. When Francisco leaned over the edge to fish her out, Kit couldn't resist—she gave him a little push, and then, not wanting to be the only dry person, Kit jumped in as well—skates and all.

Afterwards, they'd collapsed onto the grass, thoroughly drenched and laughing their heads off.

Francisco pronounced it the highlight of his

trip, and to celebrate the occasion he bought them each a hot dog and a silver balloon that had "I Love N.Y." written across it.

By the time Kit and her mother returned to the apartment, sunburned and exhausted, Kit was nearly convinced that her decision to spend the summer with Francisco was the right one.

She hadn't mentioned it to Janice yet; she was waiting for just the right moment. She'd told Francisco, though. His response had been to smile and shrug, as if he'd been sure of it all along.

"Are you next?" the girl seated beside Kit whispered. She was a slender, regal-looking black girl from Brooklyn. Her name was Lenita Johnson.

Kit nodded, too paralyzed with panic to speak. She tried to smile, but even that didn't come off too well.

Lenita patted her arm. "I know how you feel, girl. I couldn't get a thing down me this morning, and now my stomach's growling so bad I can hardly hear the music!"

Kit reached into her tote bag, where she kept a towel and a container of talcum powder to sprinkle on the bottoms of her feet. She pulled out the Hershey bar she'd stashed there in case of an emergency, handing it to Lenita.

Lenita flashed her a grateful grin as she peeled back the wrapper. It was just the distraction Kit had needed to ease the tension.

111

When they called her name, she stood up. She still felt nervous, but at least she wasn't petrified.

Kit walked over and handed her cassette to the woman operating the tape deck. She'd chosen music a little bit off the beaten track, as far as dancing was concerned. It was Scott Joplin's "Maple Leaf Rag."

She positioned herself in the center of the floor. Her heart was pounding, and her mouth was so dry it felt like cardboard. For a second, she closed her eyes, conjuring up all the times she'd practiced this number in Mrs. Rosen's studio. All the times she'd sweated and strained . . . doing it again and again until it was as close to perfect as she could make it.

Please don't let me blow it! she prayed.

The music began, slowly at first. Kit could feel her body easing into the rhythm the way a swimmer gets used to the water, a little bit at a time. As the tempo picked up, her movements became faster, more energetic.

She leaped high into the air, head back, arms stretched overhead, her knees tucked so that her heels grazed her buttocks. From there, she spun out in a series of leap-turns, the last one spiraling down into a floor position.

Kit forgot to count time in her head. She felt herself being swept away, the music pulsing in her where her heartbeat had been moments ago. Rolling to her feet, she executed a jazzed-up imitation of a cakewalk, which brought chuckles of amusement from the audience. She followed it by a split-leg jump.

That was when it happened. Somehow, coming out of the jump, she landed wrong. Her ankle buckled underneath her.

A flash of pain sliced up Kit's leg as she crumpled onto the floor. There was a stunned moment—a moment in which no one moved and the music jingled on, like a piano playing at a party where the guests have all gone.

Then all of a sudden everything was happening at once. The music snapped to a halt. There was a rush of murmured voices. Kit felt an arm about her shoulders, and looked up to find Lenita crouched over her, her soft brown eyes full of concern.

"I think I twisted my ankle," Kit said, her voice wobbling on the edge of tears. "At least, I *hope* that's all it is." She was too stunned to do anything but sit there, rubbing her foot.

"Can you stand up?" Lenita asked.

Madame Bouchard came over, too. She circled about Kit like an aged butterfly in her flowing orange caftan.

"Shall I call a doctor?" she wanted to know.

"N-no," Kit stammered. At this point, she was more humiliated than hurt. "I don't think it's broken. It'll probably be okay once I soak it."

With Lenita's help, Kit managed to hobble over to the sidelines.

113

"Hey, that was some finale," said Lenita in an attempt to cheer her up, "You can bet on one thing—nobody here's gonna top that!"

Kit gave her a shaky smile. Inside, she felt like crying. All that held her back were the last remnants of her shattered pride. Even after one of the judges came over to tell her they could reschedule her audition for tomorrow, if her ankle was better, Kit felt bereft.

God, she'd really blown it this time! She would never get into Juilliard now. Even if by some miracle her ankle was healed by tomorrow, there was still no way she could compete. Her nerve had been hopelessly shot.

Kit handed the cab driver a five dollar bill when he dropped her off in front of the apartment building. She didn't even wait for the change; she just wanted to get upstairs as quickly as possible. Her ankle was really throbbing.

Inside the lobby, she hobbled over to the elevator, wincing with each step. She punched the button for her floor, and the door slid shut with a thump.

Kit hoped her mother would be home. Even if they didn't get along perfectly a hundred percent of the time, Janice was always great when something like this happened. She would be right there with ice packs and a sympathetic ear for as long as Kit needed her.

The elevator jerked to a halt, and Kit fished

the extra key Ginger had given her from her tote bag. She unlocked the door to the apartment and limped inside.

Kit stopped abruptly at the entrance to the living room, as if she'd slammed head-on into an invisible wall.

There was Janice . . . *with Francisco*!

She felt as if the room had suddenly become a vacuum, sucking all the air out. She couldn't breathe. She even forgot the pain in her ankle.

Kit could only stare in frozen disbelief. They were standing by the window, framed in sunlight so that their figures were no more than silhouettes. Francisco had his arms around Janice.

God, they were actually kissing!

Kit gasped as if she'd been punched in the stomach. She couldn't believe this was happening. God, how *could* she? *My own mother.* It was like a bad movie she couldn't switch off. Hot tears blurred the scene before her, stinging her eyes.

Ignoring the pain in her ankle, Kit whirled around and began running back down the hallway. Through the pounding in her ears, she heard her mother cry out, "Kit . . . wait!"

But Kit didn't turn around. She never wanted to see her mother . . . or Francisco again as long as she lived.

Chapter Ten

Kit didn't know how long she'd been sitting on the park bench. She was so wrapped up in misery, she was oblivious of everything else. When the lengthening shadows of the trees finally enveloped her, she looked around, surprised to see how dark it had gotten. It was getting chilly, too. She shivered, wishing she'd brought a sweater.

Across from Kit on another bench sat an old woman bundled in rags. Next to her on the grass was a crinkled shopping bag that looked as if it were stuffed full of old clothes and empty soda cans. She was breaking off bits of a stale hot dog bun and tossing it to the pigeons.

"No fighting, boys, no fighting," the old woman scolded the pigeons in a shrill, cracked voice. She pointed a bony finger at the biggest one, a sleek gray bird with iridescent green wings. "No more for you, Ernest. You're fat enough as it is. Save some for the others."

That's me in fifty years, Kit thought dejectedly. I'll be sitting on a bench, old and gray, pretending a bunch of pigeons is my family.

A tear slid down her cheek. She brushed it away with an angry jerk of her fist. At least those pigeons wouldn't turn on her the way her own mother had.

This was the worst thing Janice had ever done—worse than the time she'd missed Kit's first big dance recital because of a date with Hugh; worse than the night Kit had waited a whole hour in the rain for her mother to pick her up from a school dance, and Janice never came—she was so busy with Doug, she'd forgotten all about it.

There was a sick, cold feeling in the pit of Kit's stomach as she relived the scene with Janice and Francisco. It was unbelievable. Her *own* mother and Francisco! She should have seen it coming, the way Janice acted around men, but somehow she'd never thought Mom would try flirting with her own boyfriend. It was worse than unbelievable . . . it was positively *gross*.

And if Janice's betrayal wasn't enough, there was Francisco's. Kit realized she'd been foolish to think he cared about her. All that talk about butterflies and love . . . probably the only time he thought about her was when he was actually with her. She understood now why she'd always had that funny half-afraid

117

feeling whenever she was with him. Sure, he was handsome and exciting, but . . .

Francisco reminded her of something that had happened to her when she was about four or five. She'd been over at her grandmother's house, looking at the angel chimes Nana brought out every year at Christmastime. Fascinated by the miniature carousel of bright brass angels whirling above the candle flames, she'd reached for one of the angels, burning her hand in the process.

In a way, that's how it was with Francisco, wasn't it? She'd been so mesmerized by his flashy looks and personality, she hadn't let herself see what he was really like below the surface. As a result, she'd gotten burned.

An image of Justin popped into her mind—his serious, angular face and calm gray eyes. Even when he made her mad, she'd known she could depend on him. He was solid and reliable the way an oak tree is solid, with both feet planted firmly on the ground. She'd felt secure with him in a way she never could have felt with Francisco, who was so busy flitting around like a butterfly he probably didn't even notice it when he'd hurt someone. Justin wasn't flashy or impetuous or poetic, but . . . well, he was *real*.

Francisco was more like a fantasy. She couldn't even feel too angry at him. He was like a dream person who evaporates when you wake up. And that was exactly what she'd been doing with Francisco—dreaming. She'd wanted to prove how wrong Justin was for being so wrapped up in his future plans that she'd jumped on the first merry-go-round that came along.

The trouble with merry-go-rounds was that they never went anywhere. You always ended up in the same place where you began. And the only thing you got from the ride was a dizzy feeling and a brass ring that wasn't of much use anyhow.

Justin had been right, Kit realized, the cold feeling in her stomach becoming a dull ache. Maybe if she'd been thinking more about her own future, she wouldn't have twisted her ankle at today's audition. She'd been so caught up in her activities with Francisco that she hadn't practiced as much as she should have. Those nights she hadn't gotten home until after midnight hadn't helped, either. But she'd probably blown it forever with Justin now, too. She'd acted so immature and selfish, it was no wonder he'd backed off.

The awful thing was she still loved Justin. She'd loved him all along, even if she had gotten sidetracked by Francisco for a little while. She could only hope there was some small chance of winning Justin back. It was obvious from the way he'd acted over the phone that he was completely disenchanted with her.

Kit covered her face with her hands to muffle the sob that tore out of her. "Justin," she choked softly, "oh, Justin . . ."

She couldn't remember a time when she'd been unhappier. She felt so alone . . . without even her friends to turn to. And she certainly couldn't turn to her own mother. Not after what Janice had done.

Kit would never forgive Janice for this. Not ever . . .

"Hey, baby, what's happening? You look like you could use a friend right now."

Kit dropped her hands from her face, staring in dismay at the man who had sat down next to her. He looked about thirty or so, with a pointy face that reminded her of David's Doberman pinscher. He was wearing a shiny red shirt that hung open in front, revealing the clump of gold chains around his neck.

When Kit didn't answer right away, he slid an inch or two closer. "You lost, baby? You need somewhere to stay? My place ain't far. . . ."

Kit bolted off the bench like one of the startled pigeons that scattered in her wake as she ran. Her twisted ankle exploded with fresh pain, but she didn't stop until she reached the edge of the park.

She'd heard about men like that. Once, she'd seen this TV movie about a girl who ran away to New York City. A strange man had taken her in and bought her clothes. Then afterwards, he wanted her to work for him . . . as a prostitute.

Horrified by the experience, Kit decided she'd better go back to the apartment—no matter how angry she was at Janice. New York City wasn't exactly Glenwood. According to Ginger, it was no place to be wandering around in alone at night.

Kit didn't relax until she reached the apartment building several blocks away. She limped across the lobby and into the elevator, sagging against the wall. Her ankle throbbed so painfully, it felt as if someone were pounding on it with a jackhammer.

The door was just sliding shut, when a masculine shoulder shoved its way inside.

It was David, looking blow-dried and immaculate in a blazer and skinny tie. "Hi, Kit . . . hey, what happened to you? You look like you got hit by a truck!"

It was the first time Kit had thought about how bedraggled she must look, with her tear-streaked face and hobbled foot. "Thanks," she answered dryly. "I really appreciate the compliment." She was too tired and upset to make polite conversation with David at this point.

His jaunty expression instantly melted into one of concern. "Look, I'm really sorry, Kit. I didn't mean to make you feel worse. . . ."

"Don't worry. Nothing could make me feel worse."

Kit had thought she was all cried out, but an unexpected tear slipped down her cheek nevertheless. She shoved it away with the heel of her hand.

"What happened to your foot?" David asked, staring down as she limped closer to the door.

"I twisted it."

David bent down to look at it more closely, reminding Kit of the time she'd hurt her leg at the beach and Justin had examined it so tenderly. A muffled sob escaped her.

David straightened. "Listen, I realize it's none of my business, but I happen to know your ankle's not the only thing that's bothering you. I heard your mother down in the lobby a couple of hours ago asking the doorman if he knew where you'd gone. She looked pretty upset."

"We had a fight," Kit admitted.

"I get it. You were sort of running away from home, only"—he glanced down at her foot—"you couldn't get very far."

"Something like that."

"I know how you feel. I've had plenty of fights with my own parents." David punched the button for his floor. "Hey, I've got an idea! You can hide out in my apartment for a while if you like. There's ice if you want to soak your foot. I think I've even got an Ace bandage lying around somewhere."

"Thanks, but I don't think so," Kit said, wondering if she'd misjudged him. He was certainly acting a lot nicer than she would have expected him to. "I wouldn't be very good company right now, anyhow."

122

David smiled persuasively. "I don't expect you to be. The way I look at it, you're a friend and you're in trouble. If I can't help a friend once in a while, I might as well be living on a desert island."

Kit warmed toward him. Maybe, underneath that macho act, David really was as nice as Ginger believed. Well, if that was true, it wouldn't be the first time she'd been wrong about a boy. . . .

Even so, she hesitated. What if his parents were home? She'd never met them. What would they think if they saw her now?

But when the door bumped open at David's floor, and he slid an arm under her shoulders to support her so she could walk, Kit was too exhausted to protest.

As it turned out, they had the apartment to themselves. David said not to worry—his parents had gone out to dinner and then on to the opera, so they wouldn't be back until late.

Kit sank down on the couch. It was white, like everything else in the living room—which was nearly as stark and sterile-looking as a hospital room. Oh well, she thought, a hospital room was what fitted her mood right now so it didn't matter.

David went into the kitchen, returning a few minutes later with a plastic pail full of ice water and two bottles of beer.

"For your foot," he said, plunking the pail down in front of her on the snowy-white carpet. Then he handed her one of the beers. "For your head. Doctor's orders."

"Thanks." Kit eased her foot into the freezing water. It might not do any good, but at least the cold numbed the pain. But she only set the beer down on the glass coffee table in front of her.

David dropped down beside her on the couch. The apartment was quiet except for a soft whining sound coming from one of the other rooms.

David grinned. "That's Rudy. He doesn't like locks or leashes. You should see him when I take him for a walk, a real lover-boy—he goes after every girl dog he sees."

Kit shuddered, remembering the awful man in the park.

"Cold?" David asked. "Do you want a sweater or something?"

"No, thanks. I'm okay."

David slipped an arm about her shoulders. "I learned in this survival class I took last summer that the best thing for you when you're in shock is body contact."

Kit was growing more uncomfortable by the second. She wished she hadn't come here and was beginning to think that David wasn't the Good Samaritan he'd seemed to be in the elevator. She wanted to get up, but she was pinned between David and the couch arm, with the bucket in front of her.

Instead, she withdrew by stiffening her

whole body. "I'm not in shock, I just twisted my ankle."

"You should see yourself. You're white as a sheet."

"It's this room. It makes everything look white."

"Nice, isn't it?" David glanced about proudly. "It's great when my parents aren't around, then I can pretend I'm living here alone. A real bachelor type, like Hugh Hefner. You know, I can really get into it when I'm in the mood." He squeezed her arm to show he was in the mood now.

"I think I should go now," Kit said. "This wasn't such a good idea."

She attempted to struggle to her feet, but David only clamped his arm more tightly about her. "Relax . . . I don't bite. What are you getting so jumpy about?"

"I just think I should go, that's all."

"You just got here. Anyway, what about your mother? I thought you didn't want to see her?"

"She's probably going crazy calling the police or something. I should at least let her know I'm okay." Kit began to panic when David showed no sign of relaxing his grip.

"Is it Ginger?" he asked, his light blue-green eyes probing hers. "If that's it, don't worry. She's not my only girl friend. I date other girls, too."

For some reason, his confession didn't surprise Kit, it just made her mad.

125

"What about Ginger?" she demanded. "*She* thinks she's the only one."

David shrugged. "I didn't want to hurt her. Anyway, I've been thinking of breaking it off. Ginger's not really my type. I go for more experienced women." *Like you*, his look said.

Kit saw the kiss coming, but she couldn't avoid it fast enough. Before she could worm from his grasp, he'd grabbed her with both arms, pinning her against the back of the couch in a hard, unrelenting kiss. Kit could hardly breathe, much less break loose.

He wasn't just kissing her—he was sort of *mashing* his mouth into hers in what was more of an assault on her gums than anything else. Obviously, he'd watched too many Clint Eastwood movies.

Kit broke away from him in a single violent motion. "You . . . jerk!" she cried.

She lurched to her feet before he could grab her again. Then, without thinking, she grabbed the bucket of ice water and dashed it over him.

David froze, wearing a stunned look. He didn't look so handsome anymore with his blow-dried hair plastered against his forehead in wet spikes and water dripping from his face. Then his face got very red, his expression turning from one of surprise to one of fury.

"What did you do that for?" he yelled. "Do you know how much this couch cost my parents? *Two thousand bucks!* What if it's ruined? Who's gonna pay for it?"

Kit paused to look back at him as she was limping toward the door. "Why don't you send me a bill?" she said sweetly. "*After* you tell your parents how it happened."

When Kit walked into the apartment upstairs, she found Janice by the kitchen phone, slumped on a stool with a mug of coffee in her hand. When she saw Kit, she jerked upright, putting the mug down so abruptly that some of the coffee slopped over the rim onto the butcher-block counter.

Kit and her mother stared at each other without speaking for a long, charged moment. Janice looked as if she'd been crying. Her eyes were bloodshot, with mascara smudged underneath them. She was wearing a blue chambray work shirt untucked over her jeans, and her honey-colored hair had been hastily pulled back into a ponytail with a rubber band. Several long wisps trailed forlornly down about her neck.

Kit felt torn. She was still angry at Janice, but at the same time she couldn't help wanting to run to her mother and burrow into her arms, the way she used to as a child. *Why couldn't she ever keep her emotions straight?* Kit wondered, on the verge of tears again herself.

Janice was the first to break the silence. "Miriam and Ginger are out looking for you," she said. "I wanted to stay by the phone in case you called." Her voice caught. "Oh, honey, I'm so sorry about what happened! I know how much you like Francisco. I liked him, too."

"Yeah, I could see," Kit choked.

"Not that way. You don't understand. What you saw . . . well, it wasn't what you thought."

"It seemed pretty obvious to me."

Janice sighed, hooking a loose strand of hair behind her ear. "It's hard to explain it with you glaring at me like I'm some kind of murderer. Please, Kit, will you just listen for a minute?"

Okay, Kit thought. She'd hear Janice's explanation, but that didn't mean she had to forgive her. "I'm listening," she said, crossing her arms over her chest.

Janice took a deep breath. "I know what it looked like . . . but believe me, I was just as surprised as you were. I didn't invite Francisco to come here—he just showed up. He said there was something he wanted to talk to me about—something about a trip he wanted you to take with him this summer."

"I was going to tell you. I just hadn't gotten around to it."

"Well, I was pretty surprised, as you can imagine. I think Francisco figured it'd be easier for him to talk me into letting you go than it would be if you asked. He must have seen me more as a friend than some intimidating mother figure."

"I guess he was right, huh?" Kit said coldly.

Janice flinched. "Okay, I suppose I had that coming. I know that sometimes I act . . . well, not quite my age." Her chin quivered. "It's just that I hate the idea of being *old*. Your grandparents were forty-two when they had me. They were almost sixty when I graduated from high school. I could never bring my friends over, because Dad was always sick. The house smelled like medicine. God, I hated that smell! And I hated myself even worse for being ashamed of two people I loved more than anything in the world."

Kit was startled by her mother's confession. It was the first time Janice had ever told Kit how she felt about her parents, who had died when Kit was really young. She never knew, for instance, that Janice had been ashamed of their being so old. Even though the problem was just the reverse for her, Kit couldn't help sympathizing with the way her mom must have felt.

"Maybe I even led him on without realizing it, I don't know," Janice went on quietly. "What I *do* know is, when he kissed me, it came as a complete shock. I don't even think *he* planned it, not before he came over, anyway."

Knowing how impulsive Francisco was, Kit wouldn't have been surprised if Janice was right. "He's big on spur-of-the-moment things," she replied bitterly.

The tears in Janice's eyes spilled down her cheeks. "Kit, I love you. I admit I'm far from being a perfect mother, but I would never do anything to hurt you."

Kit felt her anger melting. What her mother said was true. Whatever thoughtless things she'd done in the past, Janice had never lied to her . . . or purposely tried to hurt her. In some ways, Janice was a better mother than a lot of other kids' mothers Kit knew. Since she was so young-thinking, Mom really knew what it was like to be a teenager. She was also an expert on broken hearts.

Besides, what had happened to Kit just now in David's apartment had shown her how easy it was to find herself in a situation that was not what it appeared. If Ginger had walked in on them while David was kissing her, it would have looked pretty bad, too.

"I believe you, Mom," Kit said with a sigh, limping over to where Janice sat. "I guess I knew all along what kind of a person Francisco was, only I just didn't want to admit it."

Janice jumped up off her stool. She was staring at Kit's foot, which she'd only just noticed.

"It's okay, Mom," Kit reassured her shakily. "I think it's only twisted."

"How did it happen?"

"At the audition. I . . . . I landed wrong on one of my leaps."

"Oh, Kit . . ." Janice put her arms around Kit, hugging her tightly. Suddenly, she was in command again, a full-fledged mother, as she led Kit toward the bedroom. "I want you to lie

130

down. I'll get you some aspirin and an ice-pack. As soon as Miriam comes back, I'm taking you to the hospital for X rays."

"But . . ."

"I don't want to hear any arguments, either," Janice interrupted with mock sternness. "Who's in charge here?"

Kit fell back onto the extra bed in Ginger's room with a sigh. In a weird way, despite the pain in her ankle, her disappointment over blowing the audition, and everything that had happened since, she felt strangely content.

Kit looked at her mother, who was smiling down at her with her eyelashes all stuck together in wet clumps, and felt a wave of love. She raised an invisible microphone to her lips.

"Here she is, folks, starring in the major role of her career—*my mother* . . ."

Chapter Eleven

Kit gritted her teeth as she put her weight down on her injured foot. Okay, so it still hurt a little. Was she going to let a small thing like that stop her? No. She'd made up her mind. She wasn't going to give up. She was going to complete her audition if it killed her.

"It's a question of responsibility," Madame Bouchard was explaining. "If something should happen . . . something really serious, that is . . . it would reflect badly on us."

"I'm really okay," Kit replied. "My mom took me to the doctor for X rays, and he said nothing was broken." At least that part was true. "I'm only wearing the bandage for support. My ankle hardly hurts at all."

They were standing near the entrance to the dance studio, while kids in leotards streamed past. Some of them paused to give Kit a curious glance. Kit's cheeks burned. She could see

132

she was already famous as the girl who'd blown it at yesterday's finals.

Madame Bouchard wrinkled her forehead. "Well, if you're sure it doesn't hurt . . ."

"Can I go first?" Kit asked, not wanting to sit through hours and hours of worrying herself sick. "I mean, just in case it starts to hurt later on."

"Under the circumstances, I don't see why not." She consulted the list of names attached to her clipboard, extracting a pencil from behind her ear to write Kit's name in on top. "*Voilà*, Miss McCoy. And good luck this time."

Right, Kit thought. *I'm going to need every bit of luck I can get!* She waited by the door, stretching and warming up outside in the hallway until it was her turn to go on, praying she would at least make it through her number. Even if she didn't win a scholarship, at least she would know she'd tried her best.

When it was time, Kit walked slowly toward the center of the room, with its rows of folding chairs and faces, some expectant, some openly dubious. She concentrated hard so she wouldn't limp.

She caught sight of Lenita in a tie-dyed T-shirt and jeans, sitting near the front. She flashed Kit a grin, giving her a thumbs-up signal of encouragement. Kit managed a faint smile in return.

It was obvious from the heightened murmuring of the audience that they were whis-

133

pering about her. Kit couldn't hear what they were saying, though. Her heart was pounding like crazy, filling her ears with a sound like crashing waves.

Then the music started.

Kit began to dance.

Miraculously, the pain in her ankle ebbed. It was still there, of course, but it had receded to a tiny point in the back of her mind. She was aware only of the glorious rush of energy dancing gave her.

She could hear Mrs. Rosen's voice inside her head: *"Reach . . . reach for the sky!"*

Kit stretched her body to the limit and beyond . . . jumping higher than she'd ever jumped before . . . whirling faster . . . leaping farther . . .

The piano music jangled to a frenzied crescendo. Here was the real test—a series of pirouettes, with her hurt ankle taking the full weight of the turn. Kit didn't hesitate a beat. She threw herself into the movement, ignoring the distant pain signals her brain was transmitting.

Around . . . and around. The figures seated around her in their bright-colored leotards melted into a blurred rainbow. The rushing sound in her ears became a thundering roar.

With the last turn, she dropped to the floor for her finale—something she'd planned as a surprise break-away from the traditional moves of modern dance and ballet. There was a gasp from the crowd as Kit spun about on her back like a top, knees tucked against her forehead. It was a break-dance move she'd been practicing ever since seeing *Flashdance*.

As the final chords of the "Maple Leaf Rag" sounded, Kit spun to a halt in a full sitting split, back arched, arms lifted high overhead.

Kit had hoped for polite applause. Nothing could have prepared her for the enthusiasm of the audience as they rose to their feet clapping and cheering. It echoed off the bare walls and caused the scuffed floor beneath her to vibrate. Kit was overwhelmed. She hadn't expected anything like this . . . especially from kids who were competing against her. Even Madame Bouchard had cracked a smile, she noticed. The judges were busy scribbling notes on their clipboards.

Tears of happiness blurred Kit's vision as she rose to her feet. The pain in her ankle had returned, but this time she didn't mind it so much. It was a reminder of how hard she'd fought for this moment of glory.

She knew then that it didn't even matter if she won the scholarship or not. What mattered was that she hadn't given up.

"Kit . . . wait. Can we talk?"

Francisco caught up with her as she was leaving. Kit paused on the steps, pushing her sunglasses on top of her head. She leveled a cold glare at him.

She'd been aware of his presence throughout most of the afternoon; she'd even watched him dance. He was brilliant, of course. But now, up close in his jeans and sweat shirt, he didn't dazzle her. He seemed . . . well, ordinary. He'd lost the power to take her breath away.

"I don't see what we have to talk about," she said.

"I feel I must explain . . . about what happened yesterday."

"You don't have to explain anything. I know what happened."

"Yes, I won't deny it. But you must know . . . it was not something I intended to do." He shrugged. "Who knows how these things happen sometimes? A smile, an innocent touch that leads to not-so-innocent thoughts. Perhaps it was the light, the way it was shining on her hair." He reached out and brushed his fingers over Kit's curls. "Your mother, she reminds me of you, Kit."

Kit believed he was sincere, that he probably hadn't intended to kiss her mother . . . but she also knew that, in similar circumstances, she would never have given in to her impulses the same way. Neither would Justin.

"If people went around doing whatever they felt like all the time, the world would be in an even bigger mess than it already is." She fixed him with a long, cool stare. "I thought I wanted to be more like you, Francisco . . . but I guess

136

I don't, after all. I think I'd rather be who I am."

"You're still angry, I see," he said. "Perhaps tomorrow would be a better time to talk, no?"

Kit shook her head. "No. I think it's better if we just say good-bye." She slipped her sunglasses back onto her nose. "I'm not angry. I was at first, but I'm not anymore. Anyway, I'm leaving tomorrow. I'm going back to California."

He touched her cheek, his face full of genuine regret. "I will miss you, Kit. You are so beautiful. The way you danced today . . . it was like something out of a dream."

"It was," she said. "But I can't spend my whole life in a dream. That's why I can't go to Europe with you this summer."

He frowned. "You are saying this because of your mother. I told you—it meant nothing."

"No, it's not because of Mom. It's because of *you*. The way you are. It just wouldn't work."

Francisco gave another one of his famous shrugs. His dark eyes shone with regret, but there was a smile curling up the corners of his full mouth.

"Perhaps you're right. Still, it would have been fun."

"Anyway, I never told you," she said. "Traveling make me nauseous. Any kind—cars, boats, planes. I wouldn't be much fun. I'd probably spend the whole summer with my head in a bag."

Francisco laughed. "Who knows? Maybe we

will meet again in September."

"Maybe. We won't know until they send the notices out."

Francisco leaned over to kiss her, but Kit took a step backward, keeping her distance.

Francisco shrugged. "Good-bye, my butterfly."

"Good-bye, Francisco."

Kit watched him saunter off, headed for his next adventure. Halfway across the Lincoln Center plaza, he quickened his step and began to whistle a tune. By the time he gets home, he'll have forgotten me, she thought.

The funny part was, even though she thought she should, Kit couldn't bring herself to hate him. He wasn't really mean or devious. In a lot of ways he was just a boy who didn't want to grow up. But you couldn't spend your whole life flying around like Peter Pan, she thought. Someday you had to come down to earth.

Kit was just glad she'd survived her own crash landing.

Chapter Twelve

"I wish you didn't have to go," Ginger sighed. "Ever since Renee moved out, it's been pretty lonely. Having you here is like having a sister my own age."

Kit paused in the midst of wedging a pair of shoes into her suitcase, which lay open on the bed. She'd been so busy packing, she hadn't stopped to think about the fact that she was really leaving. Now, looking over at Ginger, who sat cross-legged on her bed toying with an old frayed softball left over from her tomboy days, Kit realized how much she would miss her cousin.

She went over and sat down next to Ginger. "If I come back in September, you'll be sorry," she teased. "I'll have to borrow all your clothes to look like a real New Yorker."

Ginger laughed, glancing down at the front of her baggy turquoise T-shirt. "On you, this

139

would look like a different shirt. I guarantee it." She grabbed Kit's hand, her hazel eyes dancing beneath the froth of reddish curls that dipped over her forehead. "Oh, Kit, I hope you *do* come back in September! It'd be just great having you live here. Especially since I'll be going to Columbia, so I won't be away at a dorm. We can have our own dorm right here!"

Kit was touched. "You really mean that? Even after the way things got messed up between you and David because of me?"

Kit had told her cousin about the incident with David. She'd decided it would be better for Ginger to know the truth about her boyfriend before she made a mistake that she might regret later. Ginger had been pretty upset at first, but they hadn't talked about it much since. Kit was worried that Ginger blamed her partly for what had happened.

"I'll admit, I'm not too happy about it," Ginger confessed, staring down at the softball she was twisting around and around in her lap. "Part of it is, I feel like such a fool. I mean, I loved him, and I really thought he loved me! All those times we almost . . ." She paused, her freckled cheeks flooding with color. "Well, I guess it's a good thing we didn't, or I would feel like an even bigger fool."

"You don't have anything to feel foolish about," Kit told her. "Look at it this way—if you *hadn't* loved him, wouldn't it have been a lot worse . . . like you were just using each other? Isn't it better to love the wrong person than to fool around with someone you don't love at all?"

"I guess I never thought of it that way," Ginger said, looking up at Kit. "Anyway, the truth is, I'm sort of relieved not to have all that pressure on me. David was always bugging me to go all the way and—well, if we *had*, I never would've known if it was my decision or his. When it happens for me, I want to feel I really have a choice. And I want it to be special—the way it was with you and Justin."

At the mention of Justin, Kit's spirits sank. It made her so sad, thinking it might be over between them. She'd missed him so much this past week—more than she'd ever expected to. Kit wished with all her heart that she could start over again . . . take back the awful things she'd said. She didn't really think Justin was selfish for taking a summer job; she'd just been hurt at the time.

The problem with being close to someone, Kit thought, was that sometimes you got *too* close. You lost your perspective. It was like looking through a microscope. The other person's faults were magnified, and you lost sight of all the good points.

That's what she'd done with Justin. She'd zeroed in on the one time he'd disappointed her, forgetting all the rest—all the tender moments they'd shared, all the ways in which he'd shown his love in the past.

Now it was too late. Instead of too close, they were too far apart.

"The trouble with choices when it comes to boyfriends," she said, "is that you sometimes make the wrong ones."

"You mean like Francisco?" Ginger tilted her head to one side in an expression of sympathy. "Did you and he ever—"

Kit shook her head. "I couldn't. Even before what happened with him and Mom, I realized I wasn't really in love with him. It just seemed that way at first." She smiled. "I guess you could call it sort of an optical illusion."

Ginger sighed deeply. "God, I hope I'll be able to tell the difference the next time *I* fall in love!"

Kit thought about it for a minute, then said, "You get a secure feeling when you're really in love. You know, for instance, that the guy won't be turned off if you're not perfect all the time—like, if you're in a bad mood or if you do something really dumb. And you know you won't stop loving him either if *he's* in a bad mood or does something dumb."

"Do you want to know something really awful?" Ginger said. "I always hated the way David thought he could sing . . . only he really couldn't. A song would come on the radio, and he'd start singing along, real serious, like he was John Denver or something. 'Rocky mountain hiieeee . . . ,'" she sang in off-key imitation, collapsing onto her pillow in a storm of giggles. "Honestly, Kit, sometimes I could

142

hardly keep from laughing!"

"Next time you'd better fall in love with someone who likes to imitate Kermit the Frog," Kit laughed. "Then at least he won't sound so off."

"No, he'll just be green and slimy."

At that, they both cracked up. Kit laughed until tears ran down her face. It usually happened with her that way, she'd noticed—whenever she was sad, but something made her laugh anyway, it was always the kind of laughter that brought tears.

She really was sad to be going home. Part of it was leaving Ginger. But mostly it was because she knew that even back in Glenwood, she'd still be missing Justin.

Kit blew her nose. "I guess I'd better finish packing." She looked at her overstuffed suitcase in dismay. "Why is it there never seems to be enough room in a suitcase, no matter how big it is?"

Ginger jumped up off her bed. "I'll help you. I'll sit on it so you can close it."

"Thanks a lot." Kit gave her cousin's arm an affectionate sock. "It's the least you can do, since it's your fault my suitcase is so full. Remember, *you're* the one who lured me into Bloomingdale's!"

It was late at night by the time Kit's plane reached San Francisco and began circling for a landing. Kit peered out her window just as the

143

glittering horseshoe of San Francisco Bay glided out from under the wing.

Her stomach dropped. Whenever she flew in an airplane—all those times she'd flown to visit her father when he was living in L.A.—she was always afraid it would crash. Just in case, she tightened her seat belt . . . though she'd never figured out what good a seat belt would actually be in the event of a crash.

Janice leaned across her to have a look. "Isn't it exciting! When you see what's below, you can really feel how high up you are."

Kit closed her eyes, feeling slightly sick. She didn't open them again until the wheels of the plane had touched down on solid ground.

"Thank you for flying Pan Am," a stewardess chirped at her as they were leaving.

"Thank you for landing!" Kit blurted out in relief.

As she entered the terminal, Kit felt disoriented from the long flight. She looked over and saw a tall sandy-haired boy in jeans and an Op sweat shirt waiting on the other side of the gate. She blinked. Could it be? Was he really who she thought he was?

Then he spotted her, and grinned.

Kit's heart leaped into her throat. "Justin!" she cried, racing over to him. "What are you doing here?"

"What do you think?" He put his arms around her.

Kit was so stunned, she dropped her carryall bag—right on her sore foot. But she hardly felt the pain. She was in a daze of happiness that had lifted her beyond everything but the good hard feel of his arms about her.

She clung to him, wanting to stay like this forever, buried in his arms. He smelled as if he'd spent the day outdoors, like fresh air and new-mown grass. She could hear the thumping of his heart. It was almost as loud as hers.

Finally, they drew apart. Kit gazed up at him. He looked so good! How could she ever have thought she could fall in love with someone else?

A hundred questions darted around inside her head. Did this mean he still loved her? Was he willing to forgive her for the selfish way she'd acted?

Instead, all she could say was, "Your hair looks shorter—did you have it cut?"

She could have kicked herself. Why, in the most crucial situations, did she always have to say the dumbest things?

"Yeah." Justin raked his fingers through his hair. "Do you like it?"

Kit started to say, "I love it." But a funny thing happened, and the "it" came out as "you."

"I love you," she said.

They stood there, staring at each other. Kit was only dimly aware of the crowd swirling about them, the whine of planes taking off, the mechanical-sounding voice over the loudspeaker. Even Janice had faded into the background.

"I love you, too," Justin answered, his gray eyes damp with emotion. "And I'm sorry about . . . well, about everything. The summer mostly."

"I'm the one who should be sorry!" Kit broke out. "I acted horrible about the whole thing. It was really unfair of me. Also, pretty stupid. I mean, I'd rather have you for only *part* of the summer than not at all!"

"I could have told you before I accepted the job," Justin said. "The way it came out, I could see how your feelings would be hurt."

"When I talked to you over the phone, I . . . I thought it was all over."

"I thought the same thing."

"You did?"

"Yeah, you really sounded far away. Not just because it was long distance, either. I thought maybe you'd called to break up. I even had this crazy fantasy that you'd met some other guy. When you didn't say anything about breaking up, I figured you'd lost your nerve. That's why I came here . . . to talk you out of breaking up."

Kit laughed at how crazy the whole thing was. "I thought *you* were the one who wanted to break up. The reason I called was to see if you still loved me . . . if we still had a chance. But you were acting so . . . well, like you had a million other things you'd rather be doing, so I . . ."

146

Justin pulled her close again, murmuring into her hair. "It doesn't matter anymore. *I love you, Kit.* And I don't want to break up."

He kissed her then, in a way that told her how much he'd missed her. His mouth searched hers with a passionate, yet loving gentleness she'd never felt when Francisco kissed her. It was as if a stone had been dropped into the pool of warm happiness inside her, creating ripple on ripple of wonderful sensation.

"That reminds me of something I want to do."

At the sound of her mother's voice, Kit turned around. Janice stood there, beaming at them.

Kit gave an apologetic little laugh. "I'm sorry, Mom. I guess we got sort of carried away."

"That's okay," Janice said. "You just reminded me of something I want to do, that's all."

"What?"

"Call Steve." She began digging in her purse for some change. "You know, Kit, I really missed him a lot more than I thought I would." She had that dreamy look on her face that Kit knew so well. "I have a feeling about him. I think maybe this time, it just might work out. . . ."

"We'll get the luggage," Kit said. "Meet you downstairs."

She smiled as she watched her mother dash

off to use the phone. Janice would never change. Probably neither would she. Somehow, that didn't seem so terrible at the moment.

Kit linked arms with Justin, and they began walking toward the escalator.

"How did the tryouts come out?" Justin asked.

"I won't know for another week . . . but I think I did okay."

"Just okay? I'll bet you were terrific! Hey," he glanced down in consternation, "how come you're limping—did you hurt your foot or something?"

"It's a long story."

"Save it for our trip to Tahoe," he said, grinning. "We'll have plenty of time then."

Kit stopped to stare at him. "What do you mean? I thought you had to work!"

"I talked it over with Professor Krueger. I told him there was this vacation I'd been planning on for a long time, and it was really important to me. He's giving me a week off at the beginning of July."

Kit stood up on tiptoe to kiss him. "Oh, Justin, it's so wonderful, I can hardly believe it!" She was about to add, "It's just like a dream," but she stopped herself. No dream could be as good as this.

They continued on toward the escalator. "The way I figure it," Justin continued, "I'll have plenty of time to get really gung ho about

148

being a doctor once I hit college. This job is important, but being with you is important, too. I mean, we'll be graduating before you know it, and this summer may be the last time we can really be together."

Kit smiled to herself. As much as she loved Justin, she couldn't help thinking that, really, boys could be so dense sometimes.

"You don't have to convince me," she told him. "Don't you remember? That's what started this whole argument in the first place."

He laughed. "I guess I forgot."

"Just as long as you don't forget the most important thing about our trip to Tahoe," she said, squeezing his arm.

Justin looked at her, his gray eyes dancing. "What's that?"

She knew he knew what she was going to say—that the most important thing for him to remember was that she loved him—so she decided to tease him instead.

"Your toothbrush," she said with a deadpan expression.

Justin grinned knowingly. "Yeah . . . I love you, too."

Chapter Thirteen

"Boy, it's good to have you back!" Elaine exclaimed, grinning at Kit as she set down the sack of ice she was carrying. Her nutmeg-brown eyes crinkled up at the corners behind her big tortoiseshell glasses as she added, "You don't know how many times I reached for the phone to call you before I remembered you weren't there."

They had all gathered at Alex's house for Kit's welcome-home party. It had been Alex's idea to make ice cream, so each of them had brought several ingredients. Through the sliding glass door that led from the kitchen onto the patio, Kit could see Alex setting up the ice cream maker out on the lawn. It was a hot, sunny day—perfect ice cream weather. Kit's mouth watered at the prospect.

"All I can tell you," she said contentedly, "is that there's no place like home."

"Okay, Dorothy," Lori giggled. She was standing at the counter, pouring cream into a bowl. Kit thought Lori looked like an ice cream sundae herself in a fluffy white blouse edged in eyelet lace and striped pink shorts. Her long blond hair was gathered in a loose ponytail and tied with a pink ribbon.

Kit helped her steady the bowl while she mixed everything together with a big wooden spoon. "Well, believe me, I had more adventures than Dorothy ever did!" She didn't bother to go into details, since she'd already filled her friends in on the whole story over the phone.

"Maybe they'll make a movie about it someday," Elaine teased.

Elaine wiped her glasses with a napkin. She looked brighter than usual today in a pair of white painter's pants and a western-style blouse, with her brown hair clipped back with barettes on both sides.

"In that case, it would be X-rated!" Kit laughed.

Elaine's eyes popped open as she slid her glasses onto her nose. "Some people have all the fun," she sighed wistfully. "The sexiest thing that ever happened to me on vacation was the time my bathing suit top came off when I was body surfing at the beach. The worst part was, nobody even noticed!"

The three of them carried the ingredients out onto the patio. Alex had mastered the mechanics of the ice cream maker and was busy setting up a circle of redwood deck chairs for them to sit on while they took turns cranking it. In her jogging shorts and diving team T-shirt, she looked as if she were planning to turn this into an Olympic event.

"I just realized something," Alex said, sitting down in one of the chairs. She looked up at her friends, shading her eyes against the late afternoon sunlight that slanted over the roof of the house next door. "The last time we made ice cream was last summer, before Noodle . . ." She stopped, adding softly, "He always mixed chocolate chips in with his. He liked it when they got all frozen and crunchy."

Alex didn't talk much about the death of her brother, Jimmy, affectionately nicknamed "Noodle" because of his braininess, but whenever she did mention him, Kit always got the feeling he was just in the next room, about to come in and join them at any second.

"You want to know something weird?" Alex continued. "My mom and dad told me last night that they were considering applying to become foster parents. They wanted to know what I thought about it—the idea of having another kid living with us."

"What did you tell them?" Kit asked. She couldn't imagine what it would be like having a strange kid living in her house, but then she didn't think she had to worry—Janice could

152

barely manage being mother to one kid, much less two.

Alex poured the cream mixture into the metal freezer container that fitted into the center of the ice cream maker. "I said I didn't know. I mean, it would depend on the kid, wouldn't it?"

"Most kids are pretty cute," Lori pointed out. Even though she was an only child herself, she baby-sat for a lot of children. Lori was soft-hearted about practically everything, but she became almost mushy on the subject of kids. "Maybe it'll even be a cute little baby."

"Mom says it's more likely to be someone older," Alex said, her dark eyes thoughtful. "What if it's a boy whose biggest thrill in life is pulling the wings off flies? Or some dippy girl who wants to put Donny Osmond posters up all over the place?"

Kit groaned. "I see what you mean."

"What's wrong with Donny Osmond?" Elaine wanted to know.

They all glared at her.

"Maybe your parents just don't want to be stuck at home all alone after you go to college," Elaine pointed out sensibly.

Alex sighed. "Yeah, I know. I've been thinking it over. I decided to tell them it's okay. I just hope I don't live to regret it. College is still a long way off."

When the ice had been added, with layers of

rock salt in between, they all took turns cranking the ice cream machine.

"It's good exercise," Alex said.

"Yeah," Lori agreed, laughing. "You burn off
all the calories ahead of time."

After about twenty minutes, Alex peered
under the lid. "I think it's done now," she said.
"Even if it isn't, I don't think I can wait any
longer."

They trooped into the kitchen, where they
raided the cupboards and refrigerator for
things to mix in with their ice cream. Lori
found a jar of maraschino cherries and added
some to hers. Kit chose a combination of
bananas and granola. Alex sprinkled hers with
chocolate chips in memory of her brother.
Elaine was satisfied just to eat hers plain.

"Heavenly!" Lori pronounced after the first
spoonful. "I'll probably gain at least a pound,
but it'll be worth every ounce."

"At least you don't have to worry about
Perry," Kit reminded her. "He's so blinded by
love, he probably wouldn't notice if you gained
a hundred pounds."

"Right," Lori groaned. "Until he tried to put
his arms around me."

"You're lucky," Elaine said wistfully, sinking
down in her chair at the kitchen table. "I wish
Carl was as devoted to me as Perry is to you."

"What makes you think he isn't?" Alex
asked.

She bit her lip. "I don't know. It's just . . .

he's been acting sort of strange lately."

Kit put her spoon down. "Like how?"

"Well, for one thing, he started growing a beard."

"That's funny," Lori said. "I ran into him at the drugstore a couple of days ago, and I didn't notice he had a beard."

"He doesn't exactly have one yet," Elaine explained. "Mostly, it's just peach fuzz. The point is, he's not satisfied with the way things are anymore. Last night he told me there had to be more to life than computers and chess. I wasn't sure which category I fell into!"

"I'm sure he didn't mean you when he implied that his life was boring," Kit said, pausing to give Elaine's hand a sympathetic squeeze. She knew what it felt like to be ignored by your boyfriend—even if it was just in your imagination.

"I'm not so sure," Elaine replied gloomily. "Ever since Carl told me he doesn't believe it's possible to really know what love is unless you've been in love lots of times, I haven't known *what* to think."

"Being in love the first time is always the hardest," Kit told her with a sigh, thinking of Justin.

"I'll second that," agreed Alex, who had more than her fair share of heartache with Danny, too. "Breaking up is the hardest part."

"That's what us best friends are for," Lori declared, glancing about the table, "to pick up the pieces afterwards."

"Right," Kit said around a mouthful of ice cream. Glancing around the table at her three closest friends, she felt twice as glad as before to be home. She'd really missed them—in a different way—as much as she'd missed Justin. "Let's just hope our hearts stay intact for a change."

Elaine sighed, "I think that's what they call wishful thinking."

Kit smiled. "When it comes to boys, what other kind is there?"